TIME of WANT
◆BOOK ONE◆
THE TIMES TRILOGY

AMANDA BIANCO & STACIE JACOBS

Contemporary Fiction

Time of Want
Book One of The Times Trilogy

Copyright © 2015 Amanda Bianco and Stacie Jacobs

Cover Design and Formatting by Wicked Book Covers
www.wickedbookcovers.com

Edited by Allison Williams

Proofread by Christopher Sasso and Julie Masoian

"I will be yours in
times of plenty and
in times of want…"

PRELUDE

"Get OUT, It's DONE, go home!" Sam yelled. "You'll be sorry!"

SLAM! He was gone. She started to panic, felt the walls closing in. It was hot; her hands began to feel clammy. She heard a baby crying in the distance and started to run towards the sound. Run Sam run. She needed to find her baby. She stopped at a door at the end of a hallway. She reached with trembling hands to open it. The crying stopped. She let out a breath while looking around the room. No baby. Where's my baby? She searched the room; there was nothing, nothing but silence. She turned to leave and was startled by a shadow in the doorway. "Please don't go! Don't leave us!" she cried. "We need you! Daddy, don't go!" The shadow looked at her, smiled and walked out of the room. Another door slammed.

Sam ran out of the room, desperate to find her baby. "Why aren't you crying? Where are you?" Frustration started to build within her. There were doors everywhere. Each one she opened only led her to empty spaces. The crying started again. She ran through hallways lined with nothing but doors. She kept searching but nothing. Just as she was about to give up there it was, the door with the baby's name painted on it, hung with a nail. Pink with glitter letters spelling out her name.

She turned the knob slowly, and as she pushed the door open, she saw the bassinet in the middle of the room. She couldn't breathe, her heart was pounding. There was nothing else in the room, only the bassinet. The baby was still crying. "Mommy's here, Mommy's here." Just as she was about to reach the bassinet the crying stopped. She leaned over, grabbing the blanket. Sam felt tears falling from her eyes. The bassinet was empty. Frantic now, she screamed, "Where's my baby?"

CHAPTER ONE

Babe,

Had to get to the office early,

Didn't want to wake you.

See you later.

Love ya!

Samantha Bennett had woken up to almost the same note every morning for the past seven years. There it sat on her nightstand. *Why even bother writing a new one each day,* she thought.

"Recycle and reuse John." Her husband was a prominent defense attorney in New York City and was always on the go. There was always someone somewhere that needed a good defense lawyer. John was in high demand.

"That's part of the job, Sam. Most women would love to be in your shoes…your designer shoes that is," was John's predictable and snarky response to her whenever she complained, which didn't used to be often, but recently she knew she complained about his absences more and more. John had made the point that her unwillingness to understand the pressure he was under was an issue. Samantha knew there were days that John was thankful for his career and his busy schedule. And if she was honest with herself, as much as she complained, she too enjoyed some solitude, when it was convenient for her.

She leaned up on one elbow and crumbled the note.

"Time to get up I guess." Flinging the covers off, she slowly made her way out of bed. She took the note, along with the others from the past week, and tossed them in the master bathroom garbage. Grabbing the robe that hung on the back of the door, she made her way downstairs to get a cup of coffee.

Samantha stood drinking her coffee in the grand kitchen with every top of the line appliances one could hope for. She looked around, trying to recall the last time she and her husband had eaten a meal together. Samantha loved to cook. She loved watching John eat what she had prepared with such pride. He would often comment that she was a better cook than his mother. Lately they'd been eating at separate times or not at all. Eating alone was becoming second nature. On second thoughts, being alone was becoming second nature.

Watching the morning sunrise out of the kitchen window, Samantha contemplated her life and what had transpired over the last few months. *Why do I even bother dragging my ass out of bed in the morning? What's the fucking point?* In the past, Samantha had loved to stand in this exact spot and watch the sunrise in all its glory. It was here, in the early morning hours, that she held her most intimate thoughts. Often she would think about how fortunate she was for everything she and John had. But that was the past. Today Samantha was a different person. She was someone that she barely recognized and she was fine with that.

She swallowed down the last of her coffee, grateful that she was allowed to once again include caffeine in her daily routine. Samantha tried to convince herself that today would be a better day, that today she would move forward and everything would work itself out.

"Yeah, keep telling yourself that. It will be just like every other boring day!" Samantha walked over to the coffee pot for a refill.

Just as she was about to fill her mug with a little more caffeine, she noticed a moving truck pull up in front of the house across the street. The house had been on the market for about eight months without any potential buyers as far as she could tell. There had been no activity, no open houses, and no realtors coming or going. Well, it's no wonder, she thought, with the internet nowadays someone must have bought it sight unseen. And in all actuality Samantha had been too preoccupied with her own worries to care.

Watching the truck come to a complete stop, Samantha thought back to the old neighbors who had once occupied the spacious home. She missed them. Having another couple to hang out with who enjoyed the same things had been great. The couples had gotten along well and had shared a lot of fun moments. And although a lot of people avoided becoming too close to their neighbors, for fear of over-stepping the mark,

Samantha had cherished their time together and had loved having friends on the block.

Just as Samantha was about to turn away she heard the back of the U-Haul door slide open. Startled, she decided it was best not to take a trip down memory lane. After all, the past was the past and thinking about what had happened wasn't going to change anything. The Patterson's weren't coming back.

One morning Samantha and her husband had woken up and the Patterson's were gone, vanished. No word, no forwarding address. John would often question what brought on the disappearing act. Samantha had a couple of theories, but wouldn't dare share them with him. When he pressed for a reasonable explanation, Samantha would blow him off, or just answer, "John, how would I know? Probably family issues. No marriage is perfect. They did argue a lot. That seems to be the most logical conclusion to me. Maybe we weren't as close as we thought." Eventually John stopped asking and the issue was soon forgotten, at least by him.

As she was about to walk away and mind her own business, a man walked out from behind the truck. Samantha was pleasantly surprised. So surprised she stopped in her tracks and did a double take. This man standing across the street from her kitchen window was not just nice-looking. He was amazing looking. Surely, he couldn't be her neighbor. As she stood there staring, a thought came racing to her. This gorgeous man wasn't wearing the standard moving company attire, so he had to be moving in. Samantha wondered if her luck was changing.

It would be nice to have another couple in the neighborhood to get together with, she thought. Not that they didn't have their own little social network of friends that they enjoyed spending time with, but to have friends so close would be ideal. Sam thought back to the neighborhood when she was growing up. The block parties, barbeques, garage sales....such fond memories. What had happened to those days? Now it was a nod to a neighbor and half waves and half-hearted smiles. There was just silence throughout the day since the Patterson's had vanished.

All Samantha felt these days was loneliness.

Without noticing what she was doing, she found herself calling John. They didn't chat much during the work day due to John's schedule. Meetings with clients and being in court always took precedence. Scrolling for his name on her cell phone she figured she would have to leave a voice mail. Just as she was expecting to hear his outgoing message, John answered.

"Sam? What's up? I'm about to go into a meeting..."

"Hey, Hun, I'm sorry to bother you, but it looks like we have new neighbors. They just arrived. I was thinking maybe we should go over to introduce ourselves later."

Might as well be the welcome committee, she thought, giggling to herself. I just giggled, that's the first time in weeks. Maybe things are changing for the better.

"Sam, this could have waited. New neighbors are not exactly my top priority."

"I know. I shouldn't have called. I just thought, well, it's been a while since we made new friends and I think it will be good for us. "

"This really isn't the best time to make plans, Sam, I'm at work. When I get home later, we'll go over, ok?"

"Ok, great, maybe I should bake cookies or, oh, I know…"

"Sam, figure it out, I don't have time to discuss what to bake." She could sense the irritation in his tone.

"Ok, well, I'll let you get back to work."

John let out a sigh.

"No, it's ok. Sorry. I'm just a little preoccupied. Besides the other lawyer is running late so I have another minute." His voice softened. "I forget that you're there alone every day, especially with everything you just went through. By the way, how are you feeling this morning?"

"I'll be alright." Same question different day, nothing's changed since you asked yesterday. "Well, the doctor said to take things easy. Have you? I'm not home all day to watch so I'm going to keep asking until I know, get used to it, buttercup." She pictured him smirking.

"Oh John, stop worrying. I'm ok now, really."

We can try again soon; you just need to give your body a chance to recover."

"I know, I know, I need a fresh start. You and Dr. Simmons are a broken record. I just don't want to hear it anymore."

"OK, I'll back off for now. Besides, I see the plaintiff and his attorney walking this way. Got to go, babe. See you later."

"Yeah, bye. Love you." Samantha said to a screen that read 'call ended'.

Again, there she was, alone with her cup of coffee and nothing but silence. Even though she missed John and wished he were more available, it was almost a relief when he left for work. It was strange; on the one hand she loved him and wanted him there and on the other, even though lonely at times she enjoyed her solitude. She was a cliché. She was a woman who wanted it all: the successful husband, the nice home, the kids. She wanted to be a soccer mom; she wanted to bake cookies for the PTA fund raisers. She wanted to help with homework. She wanted the white picket fence. She wanted it all. That wasn't too much to ask, was it?

Growing up, it was just her and her mother. Her father had walked out on them when she was just a little girl. She remembered watching her mother struggle to make ends meet with dead end jobs, worrying about paying the bills and putting food on the table. They shared a one-bedroom apartment until her mother had to finally swallow her pride and move them in with her aunt.

Her mother's sister Joni was nothing like her mom. She was free-spirited, had never worked a day in her life, and never had to worry about anything. Joni had married right out of high school; her husband was Stanley Crane III, a very wealthy man. They were good people though. Joni would beg Samantha's mom Jane to stop being foolish and move in with them. They had plenty of room and her aunt wanted to help them to get back on their feet. Samantha was starting high school and the school district was phenomenal. Living with them took the burden off her mother, but the previous years had put a strain on her health. When Jane passed away a few months before Samantha's high school graduation, her aunt and uncle paid for her college tuition and bought her first car. As they didn't have any children, they treated her as their own. She was very grateful for all the opportunities they had given her.

Once they passed on, years later, she had inherited their house, the one she and John lived in today. She never wanted to sell it; the house was full of so many wonderful memories.

Samantha had made a commitment to herself, when she married, it would be to a man who provided for her family. Not some prick like her father who walked away because he woke up one morning and decided he didn't want a family anymore. And she had found a man that was everything her father wasn't. Her husband was an extremely hard worker. John was, without a doubt, a workaholic. He worked long hours and took many business trips just to provide for them. He was nothing like her old man. John was one of the good ones, always telling Samantha he would take care of her, no matter what, but these past few weeks had been so hard, recovering from their great loss. She just couldn't stand to be around him for too long.

Perhaps she was restless with so much free time. She just couldn't figure it out. Lately she was feeling that maybe he just didn't understand from a woman's perspective what a loss she has suffered. Being pregnant had been such an accomplishment for them and from the beginning John said he wanted her to be home and enjoy the pregnancy. They never thought the day would come that she would actually be pregnant after trying for so long without any luck, so to be able to stay home and get ready for the new addition was such a dream.

Well, that dream had ended. Now she felt smothered. Their hopes and dreams had been taken, not once but twice, just a few months apart. Now she was to have a 'fresh' start as John and her therapist put it. Whenever either mentioned their solution for her 'issues,' she would nod, politely look away, roll her eyes and mutter to herself, "Sure, easy for them to say."

She had been told, "Sam, you need to think positive, think fresh" so many times that she wanted to kick and scream. Who tells a grieving woman to think fresh?

Tired of thinking about her so-called short-comings, Samantha finished making the bed and made her way into the kitchen to rinse out her coffee mug. "Fresh start, huh? Where do I begin?" Placing her mug on the counter she couldn't stop herself from glancing out of the window. Curiosity made her want to take a peek. She couldn't control the temptation any longer. "Who's going to know? One quick look out the kitchen window to see what's going on wouldn't hurt."

And before she knew it, Samantha was slowly pulling the curtain back and was peering at what she hoped would be some activity across the street. At first glance there was nothing, and then she saw him.

The front door of the house across the street opened and out walked the same man she had seen earlier, tall, broad shoulders, a muscular build and dirty blonde silky hair. With a much better view she thought for a split second her new neighbor was Chris Hemsworth, the resemblance was striking. He ran his fingers across the top of his forehead to brush away a long curl from his face. He had a thin clean cut goatee, which was very sexy on a man if he wore it right, and boy, he did wear it right.. Samantha felt a little light flickering inside her. Maybe things were changing for the better.

A woman walked out of the house behind him. His wife, Samantha assumed. She was petite, with chestnut hair that was pulled back into a ponytail. Sam couldn't help but notice the baby bump. The new neighbor had to be about five months or so. Well, aren't they the perfect sight, the all American family. Isn't this great, she thought. I'm living across the street from THOR and his perfect wife and children. The life I so desperately wanted and yearned for. "I wonder what they're having," she said out loud, fighting the jealousy that was creeping into her self-conscious. "Nothing like watching the life I almost had unraveling right in front of me. Well, there you go, John, how is this supposed to help me find my fresh start?" Samantha turned from the window, then paused as a thought occurred to her. *Maybe this is my fresh start.*

CHAPTER TWO

As Samantha went about her usual routine - cleaning up the breakfast dishes, putting away the laundry from yesterday's wash, making a shopping list for the afternoon trip to the supermarket - she couldn't help but take a peek now and then to see what the new neighbors were doing. As she started to mix the baking ingredients, she wondered what he did for a living, if the pregnant woman was his wife? Would she be a stay at home mom when the baby was born? Samantha didn't notice any other children running around so she assumed this was their first.

For a moment she was lost in her own thoughts about the baby she had just lost, remembering what it felt like when she kicked or hiccupped, how active she had been. When Samantha was pregnant she would often laugh to herself that she was running out of room for the baby to grow. She was so deep in thought she didn't realize she was touching her belly, now empty. Distracted by her own thoughts, she suddenly heard a bang outside.

The moving truck door had slammed shut, bringing Samantha back to reality. Oh, no, someone was looking in her direction. Startled, she backed away from the kitchen window. Was it her new handsome neighbor? How embarrassing! Surely he couldn't see in? Act natural. Maybe pretend to be fixing the curtains. Yeah, that's natural you idiot. How could I be so obvious! Oh, Sam, you really need to get a grip. She pulled herself together and slowly walked away from the window and went back to baking as if nothing was wrong or out of the ordinary.

With the hot sun glaring there is no way he could see me. Just keep telling yourself that, you moron. Either way, close call. Too close. But for some reason she couldn't control herself. Something was drawing her to the window.

Samantha was becoming fixated on her new neighbors - or neighbor. She couldn't help but watch this extremely handsome and well-built man carrying boxes into the house. And what was the harm anyway?

The stove bell ringing in the back pulled her back to reality. "Saved by the bell. That was another close call." Samantha opened the stove to retrieve the apple pie.

"Thank God, I almost ruined the pie, I can't go introduce myself without an offering, that would be rude" plus how would she explain herself to her husband. "I was so busy checking out the hot piece of ass across the street I burned my famous apple pie that I've baked a million times, silly me. Yeah, for some reason that wouldn't work out well." Samantha laughed to herself thinking of John's reaction. How's that for fresh? She placed the pie on the stove to cool.

"Well, now all I need to do is wait for John and take an occasional peek, or two."

It was going to be a long afternoon.

Time dragged. She finished her chores and even squeezed in an early morning food shopping and had everything done by noon. She'd even prepared that evening's dinner. With all her anxious energy, she began to realize how lonely she was; perhaps she just hadn't realized it until now. Maybe I should give up my dream of having the perfect family and go back to work, she pondered. How could meeting new neighbors be so enticing to her? It wasn't as if she was meeting a celebrity. For Pete's sake, it was just a new couple. Oh, but they are new blood in town, she thought. Pounce on them quick before they get away or before they meet anyone else on this lonely desolate place called Shore Road. Still I wasn't this lonely when the Patterson's lived here, right? Oh well, can't think of them right now. I have more important things to do. I have to make a good impression.

Samantha usually kept herself busy while John was gone during the day, but something was different today. There was an excitement in the air that she hadn't felt in a long time, not since the day she had found out she was pregnant. Lately, she had felt a sudden urge to find a new distraction. Why now? Deep down, she knew why.

The past few months had been so hard on her and John. So many ups and downs, one day they were planning, the next they were mourning.

Annoyed with herself for thinking back to that awful time, she reminded herself to get with it and relax. "You just made an apple pie for the new neighbors, it's not as if you're bearing their child." Jesus, I can't even bear my own, she thought.

She found herself pacing the floor back and forth while passing a mirror, she started checking herself out.

"Hi, I'm Sam, and you are?" Samantha said to her reflection. No, that won't do, too simple.

"Howdy neighbor, I'm Samantha, pleasure to meet you." Samantha chuckled to herself as she tossed her hair and gave what John called her 'come hither' grin. Now that could work, she thought.

Satisfied with her rehearsed introduction, she went to get dressed. She chose a black silk button-down blouse with an ivory lace camisole under it with her skinny jeans. There were enough buttons undone so that there was a peek of the lace camisole showing but Samantha found herself undoing another button just to show a little more. A little cleavage never hurt anyone, she snickered to herself.

She fixed and primped her hair, making sure her make-up was flawless, checking her body at every angle she could. Not bad, she thought, at least I almost have my figure back. Hmmm, not bad at all.

Anticipation was building, what was taking John so long to get home? She was giving herself another look when she heard John's car pull up in the driveway.

Finally! John had barely walked in the door when Samantha had the pie in her hand and was pushing him out again.

"Whoa hold on, what's the rush? They're not going anywhere."

"Well, with the way people move in and out of that house you never know. We got to get them while we can." She gave him a grin. Slow down, girl; don't want him to think you're too anxious.

"Well, can I have a minute to go inside? Change clothes?"

"No, John, you look fine." Samantha grabbed his hand and laughed as they crossed the street to meet their new neighbors.

CHAPTER THREE

John knocked on the door that was already open. Within seconds their new neighbor peeked his head around to see who was there.

"Hello, I'm John Bennett and this is my wife Samantha, your neighbors from across the street. We just wanted to welcome you to Shore Road."

Samantha glared up at John. Not the way I would have introduced us, she thought, but too late now. At this point, she was annoyed with John, she tried to regain control of the conversation.

"I happened to be doing some baking and thought you might be hungry from moving all day, so I wanted to bring you a fresh homemade apple pie." Samantha was beaming with pride as she held her apple pie up to the handsome stranger. "I guess you can say we're the welcome committee." She giggled while giving her 'come hither' look. Now that's how you make an introduction, John, she thought, forcing a smile at her husband while mentally telling him off.

"Wow! Who said New Yorker's were unfriendly? By the way, I'm Derek Miller, glad to meet you both. It's not every day I get greeted with an apple pie."

He took the pie and stepped back, motioning for them to come in.

"Oh, shoot, I should have brought over some utensils and plates, how silly that I didn't think you wouldn't have that unpacked." There, she thought, if you weren't planning to invite us in to stay you have no choice now. After all, I baked this thing and waited all day to serve it up. And now that she was here in front of Mr. Miller she wasn't about to end this friendly introduction before seeing his wife.

"Lizzie," Derek shouted. "Look, honey, we have dinner! " His wife came waddling over towards them smiling and held her hand out.

"So nice to meet you! I'm Elizabeth, but you can call me Lizzie."

Cute, Samantha thought, but no real competition. Prettier than I thought from earlier, but still can't hold a candle. Stop it, this is not a competition. Again, too late she had allowed her mind to go there. Their neighbors' house was similar to their own, but it needed some updates. The old neighbors had tried their best, but didn't have the money to remodel all at once. The countertops and cabinets were dated, but all the appliances had been switched to stainless steel, which Samantha loved and had to have once they renovated their own home. John always opted for top of the line appliances because his wife loved cooking and baking; John's motto being 'only the best for his Sam,' which she never objected to.

Samantha noticed the massive amount of boxes scattered all over the hardwood flooring and the furniture that needed places to live. Great taste, but they could use a little help. Perhaps Elizabeth could use some help with decorating. Well, you have to give it to the woman, she has great taste in men, just not with furnishings. Perhaps I could assist with both. Sam, you are a naughty girl, good thing no one can hear what you're thinking.

"So, where did you move from?" John asked.

"We lived in Florida, that's where I'm originally from, but Lizzie has some family in New Jersey. When she was offered this great opportunity at North Shore Hospital, we jumped at it. She's one of the best pediatric doctors," Derek replied while smiling over at his wife who was scrambling through a box marked 'kitchen'.

"Oh, Derek," Elizabeth said.

"Well, Lizzie, it's true."

How supportive, Samantha thought to herself. "Very nice. I see you're expecting?"

"I'm just about six months so we needed to move quickly; hopefully we can get somewhat situated before the baby comes in June." Elizabeth was glowing.

"Is this your first?"

"Yes, this will be little Junior, Derek's excited about carrying on his name. He bought a little soft baseball the minute we found out we were pregnant. He was having a boy no matter what." Elizabeth winked at her husband.

"Hey, there was no doubt it was going to be a boy, I knew what I was doing while planting the seed." Everyone laughed, even Samantha.

"So what do you do, Derek?" *I bet you model underwear for Abercrombie and Fitch.* Samantha couldn't help but blush as he answered her.

"I'm a writer."

"A writer, huh? Have you written anything I would know?"

"Well, unless you're an avid sports reader, I doubt it."

"Don't let the designer outfit fool you. My wife can throw a mean curveball." John chimed in.

"Sounds like a domestic problem I'm not sure I want to know about."

"Yeah, keep it up, John. I may have to warm up my arm later!" Samantha pretended to throw a ball at her husband's head. "So I guess you're a sports writer, wise guy?"

"You got it," Derek answered, still laughing.

"My husband was a writer for the Florida Times for almost ten years. It was actually a great job, but he was always on the road. So, once we found out I was pregnant we discussed Derek's dream job. He's always wanted to write a book."

"So we decided that I would stay home with the little guy and try my hand at writing, no pun intended." They all laughed. "I guess I'm a modern guy. I'm a stay at home dad."

Samantha was intrigued. "What's the book about, if you don't mind me asking?"

"I don't mind at all. Besides, I think Lizzie is tired (
me talk about it."

"I never said that, but let's be honest, you eat, sleep _
dream about this book. But my husband is a passionate man
and never quits what he starts."

Samantha looked over at Derek who was smiling, clearly
enjoying the compliment his wife had given him. She felt his
stare linger on her a little longer than was necessary, but she
liked having his attention.

John broke in, "Hold on. Dude, you gave up great tickets to
all the great games to stay home?"

Samantha wanted to reach over and strangle him. *Thanks
John, great way to make friends, you idiot.* She was so embarrassed.

"I think my husband is still living in the 1800's. John dear,
this is not Walnut Grove. We have running water, electricity
and guess what? There are now stay at home dads! Jeez, how
obnoxious can you be?" Samantha reached over and slapped
him on the arm. "Really John…"

"I'm sorry. I didn't mean to sound like a chauvinistic pig.
Really, I didn't. It just occurred to me that you probably get
great seats. It's cool though, go for it man! But I'll shut my
mouth since I obviously have my foot in it."

Sam rolled her eyes at him. "Anyway, what were you saying
Derek?" Thank goodness John's insulting comment hadn't
seemed to bother the Millers.

"Well, it's about sports, obviously."

"Of course," Samantha replied with a smile.

"I'm exploring the idea of a mentally disabled boy with an amazing pitching arm trying to break into the world of major league baseball. What he goes through, the rejections. How he was discovered, the path he and his coach take. It's still in the working stages, but that's the general idea."

"That sounds so interesting. I can't wait to read it."

"Derek was able to get a publisher with just an outline of his book. That rarely happens so quickly. I am so proud of him." Elizabeth smiled at her husband.

"I've been lucky with some good people on my side. Now I just have to actually write it!"

"Something tells me you'll be a fantastic author. I look forward to seeing your body of work…"

They all looked at Samantha. She could feel her cheeks blush. All eyes were on her. All she could think was *Shit, did I really say that out loud? You dumb ass.* Trying to recover from her embarrassment she quickly regained control. "I mean I look forward to reading it." Everyone laughed at her expense.

"What about the two of you?" Elizabeth asked.

"I work in the upper west side of Manhattan; I'm a defense attorney," John answered.

Samantha's eyes followed Derek as he walked over to help his wife with opening the box and searching through it for knives and forks. *Attentive,* she thought. She was starting to realize that he was more gorgeous up close than from across the street. He also carried himself with such confidence. She could tell that when he walked in a room, all eyes were on him. She certainly couldn't take hers off this unbelievably attractive man.

"Oh, that must be exciting. Well, we are excited to be here," Elizabeth smiled.

"Well, you'll like it here, there's no place like Long Island and the North Shore is a beautiful place to live, we both grew up here," John said.

Derek was balancing plates in one arm and silverware in another. Samantha ran over just as the plates were about to fall out of his hands, grabbing them just in the nick of time. Derek looked at her and winked. *Oh Lord, those eyes, they were more piercing now than before.* Maybe because they were looking at her and no one else. Trying to not blush too much, she quickly turned to the island and began cutting the pie into pieces.

"That's good, now we know who to call if we need any legal advice, especially with this house. The hospital needed Lizzie to start immediately; thankfully, Lizzie's cousin is a realtor. We took their suggestion and went with this one, glad the pictures were accurate, but with my wife's personal touch, we'll soon have the house of our dreams."

Yeah, I've heard that before, Samantha thought. Breaking her from her concentration, Derek asked, "And what about you, Samantha?" John and Samantha eyed each other for a moment, not sure of how to answer the question. As simple as it was, she wasn't ready to share their private matters.

"I, uh, I'm not working right now. I left my executive job in an accounting office a few months back, and haven't decided if or when I'll be returning." *Why couldn't I just say housewife? Or I don't work?* Samantha was angry with herself.

"That's nice, do you have children?"

"No," her husband answered abruptly. There was an uncomfortable silence for a brief moment and, as Samantha was thinking of what to say next to recover the conversation, Derek's phone rang.

"Excuse me for a moment." Derek left the kitchen and headed through the living room and up the stairs into one of the bedrooms.

Omg, sexy and buns of steel, can this man be any more delicious. Pull yourself together lady, Samantha thought to herself. As Elizabeth was serving the pie, Samantha looked over at her husband who was making small talk. She had always thought of John as an attractive man, tall, muscular, light eyes and hair, a picture perfect pearly white smile. He had been very popular in high school, all the girls wanted him and all the guys wanted to be him. He was adored by everyone he met. Over the years he had aged a bit more than Samantha, but the stress of his career was to blame for that. Attraction had never been an issue with them and it still wasn't. They had never had any problems in the bedroom. Of course, after being married for eleven years, things were a little predictable but Samantha was good at keeping things alive. She had tried all the things that Cosmo suggested like sexy lingerie and role playing.

Hmmm, I wonder what kind of lover Derek is. Listen to yourself, you sound like a girl in heat. Well, maybe I am, so what? A girl can dream, can't she? Samantha could feel herself slipping into her old ways. *Not again girl.* She couldn't help it; there was something about this new man in the neighborhood. What it was exactly besides his good looks she wasn't sure, but she was almost willing to find out. No matter how she tried to fight it, from the second she had seen him she had been mesmerized.

"Sorry, that was my publisher," Derek said as he returned to the kitchen. Samantha kept trying to glance his way without anyone noticing. No matter how hard she was trying to be inconspicuous, once or twice he would catch her and give her a smile. *Could the dimple on his left cheek be any cuter?* Hoping her husband wouldn't notice, she followed her new neighbor's every move. Watching him take a bite of her apple pie, noticing how he put his fork down after each bite as if he was savoring every piece. I wonder, she thought, if he was that graceful with everything he did. She could just watch this man all night. Just as she was about to offer him another piece, John announced that they needed to get going. He had an early morning and needed to get home and prepare. And he didn't want to overstay their welcome. John, you buzz kill. Can't you see I'm not ready to leave yet? Samantha wanted to yell at him, but instead she nodded at her husband. The Millers stood up and said all the right things: great meeting you, thank you for the delicious pie. What a friendly gesture, *blah blah blah* Samantha's attention was caught by Derek, however, when he said, "Looks like some drinks are in order, what do you say neighbors?"

"Deal," said Samantha. Because she was so animated and quick with her response everyone laughed. At that moment she knew that there was something different about the Millers. She wondered if they would stay longer than the previous occupants of 23 Shore Road. Sam and John said their good nights and made the walk back home. When they reached their door,

27

John said he wasn't hungry and was skipping dinner, which was fine with Samantha since she too had no appetite, at least not for food. He went straight to his study and Samantha sat on the front porch staring at the Miller's new home, wondering what they were doing, what they were talking about. They really were a nice couple. John came to the front door and said how late it was. Samantha stood up and followed him into the house, closing the door behind her. In the master bathroom, she did her usual nightly routine of cleaning her face, brushing her teeth, laying her clothes out for the following day. This night, however, she seemed to be a little more particular when choosing what to wear. Things suddenly seemed new and fun. Distraction she thought, that's all this is. I can handle this, after all, I was told to start fresh.

CHAPTER FOUR

After their first encounter with the Millers Samantha kept a close eye on their progress, being as inconspicuous as she could. Every morning she stared out the kitchen window, hoping to catch Derek running out to get the paper or bringing in the trash cans. Any small sighting was a secret high for her, like watching a really good reality show, staring at her gorgeous, unattainable neighbor. She couldn't help it. She was becoming an addict. And the scary part was, she was having a hard time convincing herself that this was just a crush. No, she felt that this was more. This was her salvation.

Samantha managed to keep herself busy by wiping down the porch furniture, doing some landscaping, adding more flowers, garden accessories, trying to get ready for spring. She enjoyed the outdoors and took great pride in her garden. The weather was warming up and spring was in full bloom. John would argue with her that they hired professional landscapers to maintain their large property but Samantha wanted to feel useful. Besides, it was therapeutic for her and gave her a sense of calm, a feeling of importance. She had no one else to take care of, no one who really needed her. Sure, she had her husband but he was working all the time. And really how much babying did a grown man need? As her mother would say, 'Feed them and fuck them, Sam! That's all they want!' Samantha couldn't help but laugh out loud. Still, she needed more.

Normally Samantha would throw any old thing on to work in the yard but lately she was going for a sexier look; she never knew who might be looking. Today she chose a pair of fitted Capri leggings, with a tight white tank top and a thin-fitting zipper hoodie with no bra. Even though spring had arrived it wasn't quite shorts weather yet; this would be her new attire for garden work until she could break out the daisy dukes. Then Mr. Hottie across the street would have something to see. John always told her that no man with a heartbeat could resist watching her strut by with her short shorts on. *Let's test that theory, shall we? Sam, you are really digging yourself deep. Start digging out these flower beds and stop thinking about Mr. Miller.*

Derek sat in his new home office staring at a black screen. He was waiting for the words to just magically appear. He would start a sentence and then delete it, nothing seemed right. *Come on, Derek, this is not the time to have writers' block.* He picked up a pen and started to write an outline, hoping that would maybe trigger something; instead he drew a picture of a tree. *Well, at least it's a nice tree.* Frustrated, he flung the pen across the desk and twirled around in his chair. He stopped spinning and looked out the window. His neighbor Samantha was in her front yard working in her garden. Derek couldn't help but laugh at how carefree she seemed kneeling down pulling out weeds. He noticed a radio by her side; she was moving to whatever was playing. She looked like she was having a great time, while he was stuck inside working. Derek couldn't help but feel a little envious; he couldn't remember the last time he had any fun. "Speaking of work, get to it," Derek muttered to himself.

He turned away from the blinds and went back to the dreaded blank screen. What he wouldn't give to just say fuck it and go catch a movie or go fishing, but he knew he couldn't. The plan was that he would stay home and write his book, it was his new career. He had just never realized how hard the transition would be. He was used to traveling with his last job, always on the go covering games like the Super Bowl or the World Series. Derek had a flare for interviewing players; he never had to work hard on getting a good interview. Players had often commented that with Derek it was more like a couple of guys hanging out shooting the shit. Lately, the closest thing to an interview he got was talking to the cable guy inquiring about their services. Derek loved his career but he loved his wife more and he was willing to try anything to keep his family happy.

When Elizabeth was presented with the opportunity to transfer to a New York hospital, she was elated. Derek wanted to be supportive and he wanted his wife to be happy. However, Derek wasn't in love with the idea of moving. Sun and fun was his life in Florida, and with their respected careers they were able to pick up and go anywhere for an overnight trip or a day excursion. They had no one to answer to, and he liked it that way. When he tried to discuss his concerns with his wife about moving, Elizabeth already had her mind set. Her career was her baby. Derek respected her for the devotion, he loved his career too, he just wasn't happy with up-rooting their lives. He suggested they keep their town home in Florida just until Elizabeth was certain the position would work out. That would allow him to keep his job and travel back and forth for the first few months. Elizabeth didn't want to even entertain the idea; they were moving and it was final. That's when Derek had started to have doubts about their marriage.

No relationship was perfect. Derek understood that just as much as the next guy. During the course of their relationship, before he and Elizabeth married, they had their fair share of issues. They would have the typical fight over an ex-lover, over who forgot a birthday card or who didn't replace the toilet paper the proper way. After arguing they would make up, and usually ended up in bed. They had always managed to work through their issues and came out stronger in the end.

Derek and Elizabeth were a team. Together they were unstoppable. They both shared the same vision early on; they wanted to be established in their careers before starting a family. They would lie in their dorm bedroom, eating popcorn and drinking stale beer, making plans for their future. Elizabeth, the planner in their relationship, had every detail mapped out, a quality Derek had found endearing at the time. He had loved how whenever she spoke about being a doctor, there was a twinkle in her eye. She seemed so positive and focused. Nothing was going to stop her from making her dreams come true. With all Elizabeth's hard work and her driven spirit, she would be Dr. Elizabeth Parks.

"You mean Dr. Elizabeth Miller, right?" Derek would tease her, while they lay in bed cuddling.

"What makes you so sure that I'm going to marry you? I don't see a ring on this finger so I guess until then…" Elizabeth had sighed, waving her hand in his face and giggling.

"Patience, patience… I have this one covered. This is one thing you can't plan. I have this all under control. I plan on taking you to a fancy dinner at McDonalds and just as you open your dollar hamburger, I'll slip the ring in the fries. The surprise on your face will be priceless." Derek laughed.

"Don't you dare, Derek Miller! If you think that is romantic…I will kill you." She had jumped up, putting her hands on her hips, trying not to laugh.

Derek leaned up, reaching for her, "Ok, maybe Burger King instead." Just as she had been about to protest, he had grabbed her face and one thing had led to another.

Derek shared the same drive as Elizabeth; however, he wanted to enjoy life too. He appreciated that she was so organized and so on point with every goal she made. Derek, on the other hand, wanted to enjoy the college life and take in everything it had to offer. He never turned down an invite to party or a day at the beach; he was often the life of the party. He would try to get Elizabeth to let her hair down and have a little fun too, but she would say no thanks and go back to studying. Elizabeth never held Derek back from going out with the guys, but she made a habit of letting him know that he should take his school work a little more serious. At times, he felt as if he was being scolded like a child. He understood how serious she was about chasing her dream so he would refrain from getting mad and would let it go. He loved Elizabeth and knew she was the woman he wanted to be with. After dating for four years, just as he had promised, he popped the question.

Derek didn't propose at Burger King like he had teased, instead he proposed in the most romantic way he could think of. Being a baseball player for his college team had its perks, he pulled some strings and planned a romantic dinner right on the field. Just as they were finished with dessert, Derek got down on one knee and proposed. He could still remember her expression when he opened the box to show her the ring; she had been ecstatic. They had both cried. It had seemed like an eternity waiting for her to answer. When Elizabeth had finally said yes, Derek had slid the ring on her finger. He would never forget her saying, "Mrs. Elizabeth Miller," while holding her hand up, admiring her ring. It was the one and only time she didn't refer to herself as 'Dr.' Elizabeth Miller.

Marriage life had its moments. Just like any new couple they went through growing pains. They had struggles with balancing careers and married life. They always tried to make time for a date night, but with Elizabeth's internship at the hospital she would often cancel at the last minute or would have to leave early in order to get back to work. Some nights together that's all they talked about, the hospital and the patients she helped or the nurses. Derek found it hard to get a word in, but he would throw in a joke when he could. Elizabeth would giggle and apologize for taking over the entire conversation, but he admired the way she spoke about her profession. He let her tell her stories; he loved her and knew one day his time to shine would come. And it did.

While working for the local newspaper, he received the call. The call he had waited for, for what seemed forever. The Florida Times reached out to him and offered him a job. He would have his own sports column, something he had always dreamed of. Derek jumped at the opportunity and had finally felt that his time had come. He couldn't wait to get home and share his good news with Elizabeth.

When Derek had arrived home anxious to tell his wife about his new job, she was running out the door clearly in a rush. He had grabbed her by the waist and pulled her in for a big kiss. She had looked at Derek with curiosity. "What's this about?"

"Elizabeth, I have the best news! Break out the champagne… I'm the new head sports writer for the Florida Times!"

"Oh, Derek, that's fantastic. I am so excited for you, but, we have to celebrate another night. I'm sorry, I have to go. The hospital is shorthanded and they need me." Elizabeth had reached up and touched his face. "I am so proud of you. I love you and I promise we will celebrate soon."

"I understand, I really do, but can't you call them and explain that your husband needs you? You know, really needs you?"

"You know I would but this is my career. You'll understand now that you have your dream job. I promise we'll celebrate this weekend or something." Elizabeth had grabbed her handbag and left.

Derek had stood there in the foyer of their home, and for the first time in their relationship he felt alone. He knew he shouldn't have felt slighted, after all, his wife was a new doctor trying to prove herself. He took a deep breath, walked into the kitchen and grabbed a beer. "To me." He knew Elizabeth was proud of him and they would celebrate sooner than later. The following morning he had woken to find a shiny wrapped box with his name on it resting on the nightstand. He was so exhausted he hadn't heard Elizabeth come in last night or leave that morning. He had peeled back the paper and opened the box; inside was a pocket-sized journal. Derek had fanned the pages and noticed Elizabeth had written inside. She wrote that she promised she would buy him a nicer book than this one she had picked up at the hospital gift shop, but she had wanted to give him something right away. She was so proud of him and congratulated him on catching his first break. The following weekend Elizabeth had invited all of their friends and family over to celebrate.

Derek and Elizabeth's careers began to interfere with their time together. Determined to make the most of the time they did have, they planned night excursions or a day of lying in bed with old eighties movies and popcorn just like they had in college. However, spending time together was getting harder to do and they were growing apart.

Derek had felt their marriage was becoming a struggle and he'd thought that Elizabeth felt it too. He had tried to express his concerns, because he knew something had to give, but Elizabeth had just brushed it off as if nothing was wrong. He knew she would never cut back at the hospital so he tried to think of things that would help. Just as he was about to lose all hope in finding a solution to make their marriage work better, Elizabeth announced that she was pregnant. At first he was scared, but as the thought of being a father sank in, he was thrilled. As excited as he was, he couldn't help but feel that their marriage was still in jeopardy. He knew they needed to do something if they were going to make it; now more than ever.

As if fate was in their corner, Elizabeth was offered the job in Long Island. Derek had his reservations about moving but he was determined to keep his family together.

"Lizzie, I know this is important to you, your career has always been top priority. I don't want to be the one to hold you back. I've been thinking, what if I pursue my dream of writing a book while we're in New York?"

"If that's what you want to do. That could work to our advantage for a little. You can stay with the baby, while I'm at the hospital."

She didn't seem overly excited, but she didn't try to prevent him from chasing his dream either. If anything, it saved them from finding childcare for a little while. Before Derek could process the entire situation, and prepare himself, the house was sold and they were on a plane. For better or worse, they were on their way to new beginnings.

Derek sat there in his office chair after watching Samantha. She was still working in her garden bouncing back and forth, bending down digging, acting as if she didn't have a care in the world. Derek looked at the 'honey-do' lists piling up on his desk and then glanced at the unopened boxes he still hadn't unpacked. He was not going to have everything done before the baby arrived. To top it off, he was still staring at a blank screen. Feeling frustrated and a little overwhelmed, he stood up. "Fuck it. Maybe it's time to get that drink with the Bennett's."

CHAPTER FIVE

"Sure! We would love to get together! Tonight is great! See you guys later!" Good thing John had exchanged numbers with Derek the other day when they'd bumped into one another taking the garbage out. Brilliant too, that he'd thought of giving Derek Samantha's cell number to pass along to Elizabeth.

Samantha quickly ran up the stairs to find the perfect outfit. Picking out her clothes she called John to let him know about that evening's plans. Waiting for him to answer, she picked out a sexy red lace tank top with black tight pants. When John answered, she hardly allowed him to get a word in. From his grunts and a-ha's he didn't seem too excited about the get together. She couldn't blame him for wanting to just come home and relax. However, he must have sensed her excitement and reluctantly gave in. After they hung up, Sam raced into the shower to start her primping for the evening.

After what seemed like an eternity, John finally walked through the door. From the look on his face he had changed his attitude about going out. Thank God. Feeling relieved, Samantha relaxed a little, but the butterflies were really getting to her.

Thankfully John had eaten a very late lunch and wasn't too concerned about dinner; he changed out of his suit into something a little more comfortable, his jeans and a polo shirt.

"Let's go," John said. "By the way, you look amazing," he added, smacking her on the ass as they walked out the door. Samantha smiled. *I hope you aren't the only one who thinks that.*

The pub was a local 'dive' bar buried in the middle of the town. It wasn't fancy and was mostly frequented by the locals. Anyone not looking for it could walk right by and not even notice it was there.

It was a hidden gem with a pool table, dartboard and an old juke box filled with oldies from the seventies and eighties. Samantha laughed to herself that songs from the eighties were now considered 'oldies'. She and John often visited the pub for date night and always had a good time.

Samantha always liked the fact that the pub was a place where everyone minded their own business. Discretion was the pub's hidden motto, which enticed Samantha. If those walls could talk…

They planned on meeting at the bar since Elizabeth was working a little late and it was close to the hospital. Samantha and John arrived first, got a table and ordered some wine.

Anticipation was brewing within her. She was fidgety and was trying her hardest to not rip the napkins apart waiting. *Oh geez do I look ok? If I pull out my pocket mirror and check one more time John is going to freak out. He is already on the brink of slipping into a mood; better not push it, Sam.*

Trying not to watch the door for their new friends, well mostly for Derek, she watched a young couple playing pool. Must be a first date, she thought. The way the boy was showing the girl how to hold a pool cue was almost comical. The poor guy was so nervous. I don't think you're getting lucky tonight buddy. I feel your pain, she thought.

Samantha looked up and noticed Derek standing next to her, smiling. "Oh. You're here! Please sit." She stood and gestured to the chair next to her. Derek sat down and proceeded to shake John's hand. After a few minutes of small talk Elizabeth arrived from work. The two couples hit it off immediately. They felt as if they had been friends for years. They exchanged stories about how they met, their marriages and careers. Samantha was so interested in Derek and his life story. She found herself hanging on his every word. Trying not to be too conspicuous, she mentioned that she and John had been married going on eleven years. They were high school sweethearts who had dated off and on through their college years, since John's studies took up most of his time and Samantha went away for college. Once they both graduated, they tied the knot and had been happy ever since. It turned out that Derek and Elizabeth had been married for eight years. They had met through mutual friends who introduced them at a party and they hit it off. Elizabeth went to college in Florida to become a doctor and Derek caught his first big break writing for a reputable paper.

They laughed and told stories, striking up an instant friendship. Samantha and Derek had made eye contact a few times during the evening and she couldn't help but feel there was something more behind his gaze. Maybe this is what's been missing she thought, new friends. But something told her that she was in for more.

After a few cocktails, Elizabeth sticking to water and lemon, they decided to call it a night. Samantha didn't want the night to end but she knew John had to get home to bed.

"We must have you over for dinner one night,"

"We would love that! With Lizzie working so many hours, I don't know when the last time was that I had a home-cooked meal," Derek joked, winking at his wife.

"Done! I'll make a nice pot of sauce, meatballs, sausage, garlic bread. I can cook a mean Italian dinner. Let me know what night works for you," Samantha said, beaming, mostly looking at Derek for his acknowledgement.

"Ok, sounds amazing, I'll let you know."

Sam tried hard not to let her disappointment show that Derek hadn't answered. He was too preoccupied with helping his pregnant wife get up.

It's ok, Sam, you'll get him with your sauce. She couldn't stop smiling to herself as they said their goodnights.

As they drove home, Samantha couldn't help but think about the events of the evening. How Derek would tilt his head when listening to a story, how his eyes would light up when he laughed, the way he reached over and caressed his wife's neck when she yawned.

"What do you think, hun?" Samantha realized that John must have been talking and she had tuned him out.

"Think about what?" She turned to look at him.

"The barbeque next month? Inviting the Millers?"

"I think that's a fantastic idea."

"You seem to really like Elizabeth. And Derek seems like a good guy."

"I do," she replied. *Who cares about Elizabeth? It's Derek who has my interest.*

CHAPTER SIX

Life went back to normal on Shore Road. Samantha was busy with her garden, John was working more than usual and the neighbors were still settling in.

Samantha and John had made good on their offer and had the Millers over for dinner the week following their evening of drinks. They had a great time and were really getting to know each other.

Samantha would, on occasion, bump into Derek while working outside. He always walked over and they would chat. She made sure she had coffee on just so he had a reason to stay a little longer.

During his visits they would chat about anything and everything, she enjoyed listening to him talk about his love for sports and how growing up he had attended local games with his father. Afterwards, he would go home and write about them, his father was his best friend and supporter.

Samantha wished she knew what it was like to have a father who cared as much as Derek's. Her mother was her rock; she was there in more ways than Samantha could count. She wished she'd had more time with her, but she wouldn't change the relationship they'd shared.

Derek continued to talk about how his book was coming along and all these fantastic ideas he had. Samantha couldn't help but smile at how ambitious he was. Who knew ambition could look so sexy?

Yes, John was ambitious and he strived to be the best, but Derek...he had passion. She admired that about him. There were moments she almost felt compelled to open up and talk to him about her miscarriages, he was so easy to be around, but she couldn't do it, not yet. However, with each moment they spent together her attraction for him grew and she couldn't help but feel Derek was attracted to her as well.

After their encounters, Samantha found she had a little more pep to her step. Waking up in the mornings was filled with the anticipation that she might bump into Derek.

Thank God men were creatures of habit. Samantha knew her new neighbors' schedule better than her husband's. Elizabeth always left at the same time in the morning, whether she worked an early shift or not, and shortly after, the light in Derek's office would turn on. Samantha would always wait until late morning to go outside and start working on her garden.

Never wanting to look too eager or obvious, some days she wouldn't go out at all. Those days were always a little more exciting. Some days she would receive a text message, or an email with a quick howdy, what's up. They brightened up her day and made her feel wanted.

However, today was not one of those days.

Elizabeth was home. Samantha had noticed Derek leaving early in the morning and he hadn't returned home since. She lingered at the front window a little longer staring at the Miller's home until a thought occurred to her. She still had Elizabeth's spring form tray to return. Grabbing the pan off her kitchen counter, she decided now was the perfect time to return it.

CHAPTER SEVEN

Samantha knocked on the Miller's front door and peeked through the window.

"Oh hi, Sam!" Elizabeth's smiled when she saw her new neighbor and friend standing there.

"Hi, hope I'm not disturbing you? I don't want to interrupt anything. I just realized that I never returned your pan from when you guys came over for dinner. By the way, the cheesecake was delicious."

"Thank you, although, I have to be honest, it wasn't home-made, I can't bake like you. Derek still talks about that apple pie you brought over our first night." Elizabeth laughed. "Derek's out and won't be home till later, would you like to come in?"

"Oh, I don't want to intrude, if you're trying to relax while the hubby's not home."

"Relax? What is that? Please, come in. I would love the company. Derek went to meet his publisher. No telling when he'll be home."

"Well then, if you don't mind. John isn't home either so some girl talk sounds great." *And thank you for the information. Let's see what else I can find out.*

"Oh, I must look a mess. I was just trying to unpack some more boxes in the kitchen."

Samantha watched as Elizabeth self-consciously fixed her ponytail and wiped away some dirt from her pants. Samantha stood there, feeling confident in her tight legging pants and fitted V-neck t-shirt, showing more cleavage then she thought Elizabeth would probably approve of.

"Don't worry about it, you look great!" Samantha scanned the room for anything Derek as she walked into the kitchen. There on the fridge was a picture of him with a group of guy friends. Just the sight of his picture thrilled her.

"Lizzie, why don't you let me help you unpack? Looks like you have tons to do still." Samantha couldn't believe how much work was still needed.

There were dishes, pots and pans scattered all over the kitchen table. Boxes were torn open with crumpled newspaper thrown on the floor. She knew the Miller's had only been in their new house a few weeks and Elizabeth worked crazy hours on top of being pregnant. She also knew Derek was busy writing, but what was taking them so long? She would have been done within two weeks top! *Maybe I'm a little too OCD.*

"Oh, I would never ask, but if you don't have anywhere to be, I could definitely use some help in here. If I waited for Derek, all this would be done when the baby starts kindergarten; he has been helpful, but the kitchen is no place for a man!" Elizabeth chuckled and Samantha returned her smile. "Can I get you a drink, some iced tea or coffee?"

"I would love some coffee, if it's not too much trouble." Samantha began to organize the items on the kitchen table while Elizabeth put on a pot of decaf.

Within a couple of hours the cabinets were fully stocked with clean dinner plates, bowls, coffee mugs, pots and pans. The drawers were filled with silverware, extra utensils and saran wrap.

While working, the two laughed and made jokes about their husbands. Who leaves the toilet lid up and never closes the toothpaste were both common threads with each husband. They joked at how each of their spouses would leave the lights on in every room they entered but would get upset when the electricity bill came in. Their banter back and forth was fun but Samantha was looking for more. She wanted to know what their marriage was really like and what made Derek tick. She knew she needed to get the other woman to confide in her. She knew she needed to steer the conversation in her favor. And she knew exactly how.

"I envy you, Lizzie."

"Envy me? What for?" Elizabeth laughed. "You envy my disheveled look and big belly?"

Samantha laughed. "I envy how you seem to have it all - career, baby on the way, new beautiful home and wonderful husband. You make it look so easy. I would be a wreck. Doesn't help that John is always working, it gets lonely." Samantha sighed, hoping this would be enough to get Elizabeth talking. *Misery loves company. Come on, Lizzie, no one is this perfect.*

"Thank you for the compliment, Sam. But it's not always so easy."

There you go, keep talking....

"There are days I just think I can't get it all done. I feel so overwhelmed, and being pregnant doesn't help."

Boohoo poor you, get to the good stuff. "Lizzie, you do have a lot on your plate. I can't imagine what it must be like to have so much to do in such a small amount of time. But you have Derek. I'm sure he helps, no?" *I don't really care about your pregnancy, Lizzie, let's get to Derek...*

Samantha noticed Elizabeth's body relax; she seemed more comfortable with her, enough to open up, after all she must need someone to listen and Samantha was there to offer a sympathetic ear.

"I do. I do have Derek. And he is an amazing husband. But you know…"

I don't but I hope to find out soon… "Talk to me Lizzie. Tell me what's wrong."

And just like that the floodgates opened. Elizabeth poured her heart out.

"Please don't get me wrong. I am so happy for Derek and the opportunity he's been given with his book, but some days

I wish he would focus on finding a career with a new paper. I try to be supportive of his writing, but there are days I have my doubts and want to tell him to give up his dream of becoming an author and just go back to work. I'm tired with coming home to a husband that just stays at home. I'm beginning to wonder what he does all day. He claims he is so stressed with this book but I barely see anything getting done. And then he complains that he doesn't get to enjoy the things he once did. He says this book is eating up all his time. Really? He's here all day with no distractions, how could he have no time for play?"

Samantha listened intently. "Seriously? He doesn't have time for what? Going out to bars? What? Typical male, me, me, me… John is the same way at times. He wants time to go fishing, or hunting…So annoying. I feel for you, Lizzie." *I really want to be feeling Derek…*

"It must be all men. I know he gets down in the dumps being home all the time so I was thinking that it would be great for him to go to a baseball game. I thought about surprising him with tickets to a Tampa Bay Rays and New York Yankees game, but with me being pregnant and just starting at the hospital, I can't see how I can go with him. I know the game is in a few weeks but he doesn't really know anyone here yet to take my place. Besides I'm sure they're sold out by now. I guess he'll have to settle for watching it on MSBN."

"Poor baby will have to deal," Samantha said, pretending to suck her thumb and make sobbing noises. Elizabeth laughed and then began talking about plans for the house. Samantha half-listened and nodded in all the right places, not really caring. Once the topic of Derek was dropped she no longer had any interest in listening. After all, she had gotten what she came for: information.

Hmmm…Sam, make a mental note to your memory rolodex…. Tickets to a game. I think I can handle that. And I think I know the exact person to go with him. Don't you worry, Lizzie, he won't be sad anymore. I'll kiss all of his booboos.

CHAPTER EIGHT

Samantha decided to drink her morning coffee outside on her front porch swing to soak up the hot sun. Derek came out to grab the morning paper from the driveway and walked across the street to say hello. "Can I get your usual?" Samantha asked, holding up her own coffee mug. Derek happily accepted. She hurried inside to fetch him a cup. Within minutes she returned. "Here you go," she said, handing Derek the hot coffee as he sat in the white wicker chair next to the porch swing. "So, tell me about this barbeque coming up? Can John grill as good as you cook?" Derek asked smiling, showing off that adorable dimple in his left cheek. *Does he even know how sexy that dimple is?*

"Thank you; what can I say, I'm a pro in the kitchen." She moved her hand to lift the strap of her top that kept falling off her shoulder. She noticed Derek's wandering eyes and wanted his curiosity to grow. She knew it was wrong and asking for trouble, but the temptation was right there in front of her for the taking. She wanted him to want her. It was so long since she'd felt special or needed, what was wrong with a little flirting? A fresh start, the doctors and John had told her that over and over again. No one had told her where to exactly find this fresh start.

"What should we bring?" Derek lifted his eyes to meet Samantha's.

"Hmmm…I guess whatever you desire. Just having you there is enough though." She giggled playfully, giving him a little grin. "Ya know, for a man that hits a keyboard all day you have some set of guns. I'm sure you would give the single ladies something to talk about at the barbeque." She reached over and hit him playfully in the arm, testing his limits. Let's see if he plays. He laughed.

"Really? I could always show up in speedos and run through the sprinkler. And I don't just hit the keyboard. I also hit a punching bag in the basement; occasionally I hit the gym too." He was flexing his arms, showing his muscles.

"Now THAT would be a sight to see and would have the neighbors talking, speedos and a sprinkler!" Samantha was laughing hard. "Speedos, huh? I figured you were a boxer guy. But I'm sure you can pull anything off."

"How about I surprise you? And what about you? Bikini? I think you're giving the elders around here heart palpitations with your gardening attire." He put his hand on his heart.

"Funny, I was hoping it was only you that I was impressing with my clothing. After all you have a front row seat."

"Trust me, Sam, there are days when I'm getting nothing written."

"Oh, well, we can't have that. I guess I better start wearing a housecoat!"

"Don't change your attire for me. What would I have to look forward to every day then?" He hesitated. "I mean, well, you know?"

"Know what?"

"Sam, you are a beautiful woman with a great figure. Who wouldn't take a peek? I am a man after all."

"Yes, yes you are," she replied with a bashful smile. "I wouldn't want to upset my audience so I guess if there are no objections I'll carry on. Although if I am a distraction…" She trailed off again.

"Oh, Sam, you are the right kind of distraction. Trust me." He winked. Just then her house phone rang. Damn it, she thought.

"I guess I better get that. Why don't you have Elizabeth call me and I'll give her the details of the barbeque."

Derek stood, adjusting his pants nervously. Samantha glanced down and noticed a towering bulge. *Gotcha*, she thought.

"Sure will." He hesitated for a second as if thinking of something to say, but she turned her back and walked into the house. In the reflection of the front door she noticed he was checking out her ass. What a great day this was turning out to be.

CHAPTER NINE

The day had finally arrived for the Bennett's barbeque. It was only a couple of days since Samantha and Derek had their very friendly conversation. Samantha was a bundle of nerves; she had changed her outfit at least three times, hoping she had picked something that would catch Derek's attention. She had kept a low profile since their conversation. Keeping him on his toes. She didn't want to seem too eager. She had opened the door to flirtation, allowing him to know that she was ok with some teasing; however, she didn't want him to think she was dreaming about him. Of course she was, but he didn't need to know that.

Their friends started to arrive while John manned the grill and Samantha was inside preparing the salads and getting everything ready.

"Thanks for having us over," Elizabeth said, helping Samantha in the kitchen. "I'm happy we have such great neighbors. I think the move was a little rough for Derek, leaving his friends and family; he just packed up and left everything and everyone for me. Sometimes he seems a little distracted, just stares out the window watching nothing. I don't think it has really sunk in for me yet. I keep busy at the hospital all day and night. He has his writing and he's been doing most of the unpacking though. I'm glad the two of you keep each other company from time to time. It's nice to have a friend around." *If you only knew the thoughts I had about your husband, would you feel the same way?* Samantha nodded while grabbing a tray from the pantry.

"Especially with the baby coming, I know he would have liked his family around."

"Won't Derek's family visit?"

"Maybe. It all depends on his mother; she doesn't like to travel. But my parents and sister live in Jersey so at least we have them close."

"I understand. John's parents live out of state and rarely visit, and well, I don't have any family left. Everyone has passed on and I'm an only child. It sucks not having family around, but that's what friends are for." Samantha shrugged her shoulders and smiled. She brushed back her hair and started placing snacks on a tray. "It was so long since anyone lived across the street I was starting to get worried that we would never have new neighbors. But now we have you and Derek. It's funny how things work out."

Elizabeth smiled at her new friend and grabbed the platter of finger snacks to take outside. Samantha noticed that Derek was in the yard chatting with John and drinking a beer. She found herself staring at him. The blue t-shirt made his eyes pop with electricity; and the denim shorts he was wearing were snug in all the right places. Samantha felt her cheeks flush. Calm down, girl. But what was it that Elizabeth had said, that he stares out the window. *Is he looking out the window at me? Maybe he wasn't lying; maybe I'm just as much of a distraction as he is..*

"Hey, Sam... Sam? John needs the barbeque brush."

"Huh? I'm sorry, Derek, I didn't hear you come in, I zoned out for a minute. Sure, I'll get it." Samantha, a little embarrassed, walked over to the pantry closet.

"It's ok, I find myself lost in thought all the time."

"Sounds personal, what thoughts distract you, Mr. Miller?" She gave him the school girl innocent look that had melted many men in her time. Derek watched as she bent down in the pantry closet for the grill brush, her mini khaki skirt was just low enough on her hips to show the top of her panties.

"Oh, you know, beautiful views."

As Samantha went to stand up she lost her balance and fell forward onto her knee, letting out a yelp. They both laughed as Derek reached his hand out to help her up.

"Ugh, good god that hurt," Sam rubbed her knee.

"You sure you're ok?"

Samantha just shook her head in response. They stood face to face for a moment; Samantha was trying to read his thoughts. The past few weeks spending time together was fun. She was growing more attracted to him with each day spent, she hoped Derek felt the same.

"You smell really nice, what is that, vanilla?" Derek spoke softly.

Samantha rested her hand on Derek's chest. "It's called warm vanilla sugar." She could feel his heart pounding through his t-shirt, every beat matched her own; without thinking she leaned in closer and kissed him. Her lips grazed his, sending shock waves throughout her entire body. She had never experienced a kiss like that before. The whole encounter lasted for a second until Derek realized what was happening and pulled away.

"I'm sorry; I don't know what came over me." Samantha took a step back, biting her lower lip.

"No, don't apologize, it's ok really, I shouldn't have…" Derek stood frozen as his words trailed off.

Sam could see how stunned he was; she couldn't help but find it irresistible. She didn't want this moment to end. If she had any hope of finding out exactly how Derek felt about her, now was that time. She leaned in and kissed him again.

Derek didn't pull away this time; Samantha felt his hand trail down her back and grab her ass as his other hand cupped the back of her neck. Their lips parted and their tongues danced as they slid in and out of each other's mouths. A low growl escaped Derek's throat as he softly sucked on Samantha's lower lip.

Samantha grabbed his arms, pulling him closer. She was pinned up against the wall, and felt the bulge in his pants press against her pelvis. Derek trailed his kisses down her neck. She was so aroused, she wanted to tear off his clothes and wrap her legs around his waist right there. Every inch of her body tingled with desire. Samantha was lost in the moment. She could hardly believe this was happening so quickly and in her kitchen. This just confirmed her suspicion of his attraction for her; she knew that now. She wanted more, and nothing was going to stop her.

The back door slid open and Derek pulled away quickly.

"Derek, are you in here?" Elizabeth called out. "John needs the Barbeque brush."

"I...I got it, I'm coming!" He straightened his shirt and walked out, after giving Samantha one more glance. She stood in the closet for a minute longer, holding one hand over her swollen lips; she could still taste Derek's kiss. One thing she knew for sure, he was a great kisser and she wasn't done with him yet.

Walking out onto the deck, Samantha was happy to see her best friend Lauren. Lauren was a social butterfly. She could be tossed into a room of strangers and within a few minutes she would have all their names, phone numbers and addresses. The two of them had been double trouble in college. Lauren was like the sister Samantha had never had. She would normally tell Lauren everything, almost everything. But a girl needed to keep some secrets to herself.

When Lauren spotted Samantha walking out on the deck with a platter of veggies and dips, she ran over.

"Hey, lady! You look fab!" Lauren kissed Samantha and grabbed a carrot stick.

"What are you wearing? You look like you raided Beyoncé's closet!" Lauren had a cute figure and she loved to dress in true diva style. Today's ensemble consisted of black short shorts and a very low cut gold sparkle tank top and high heels. Lauren liked to make a fashion statement and a barbeque was no different. Only Lauren.

"You like? I think it says if you like it put a ring on it!" They both laughed so hard Samantha snorted.

"Classy, Sam, Classy."

"Whatever! Who the hell are you wearing that for anyway? Is there a new victim I don't know anything about?" she asked, keeping an eye on Derek who was standing by the grill talking to John.

"Nope, no one. Single and ready to mingle. By the way, who is the hottie by the grill? And I'm not referring to John."

Samantha laughed. "Oh, that's my new neighbor, Derek. Pretty nice guy." *And a damn good kisser.*

The barbeque was in full swing. They had only invited a small group of friends; people whom Samantha thought would mingle well with no drama. That was until the backyard gate opened and Vinny came walking through with a twelve-pack on his shoulder. Vinny. Well, there goes my drama free party, Samantha thought. One of John's buddies, Vinny was a fun guy. Some would say a little too fun at times. He and John had known each other for years and always had a great time together. He had also had a short romance with Lauren a few years back. Nothing too serious but when Lauren had gone to surprise him at his apartment with dinner…well, she was the one surprised.

As if on cue, Lauren dashed to Samantha. "What the fuck is *he* doing here?"

"I'm not too sure. John didn't tell me that he'd invited him. And trust me, I am going to kill him for this."

"Looks like he came alone. Good. Cheating bastard." Lauren's voice was growing louder.

"I know he was an ass. But Lauren, you weren't a couple. You were just hanging out. Can't you give him a chance? Let him apologize. I know for a fact he asks John about you all the time. I think he realizes he made a horrible mistake."

"NO! Once a cheat always a cheat!" Lauren crossed her arms and gave Samantha a tight-lipped smile.

"Is it really cheating if there's no commitment?"

"YES! It's called honesty. Obviously he wasn't happy with the way things were going, but he should have told me. I know you're the queen of breaking hearts and have never been cheated on, but when it happens to you, right in front of you…I just can't." Samantha noticed Vinny was looking in their direction.

Sam, think quickly before your new neighbors witness a homicide. Besides she didn't want to lose track of Derek or lose his interest. Samantha had different views about cheating, views that she and her best friend obviously didn't share. Just as Samantha was about to make a diversion and get her Lauren to the other side of the party, Vinny came walking over. She nudged Lauren and whispered "play nice" in her ear. Smiling,

Samantha opened her arms to give him a hug. "Vin, you dirty bastard, I had no idea you were coming."

"John called and invited me a few nights ago. He said it was a small barbeque and to stop by and grab a beer. I hope that's ok." He was looking at Lauren who was looking at him like he smelled of dirty socks; then she turned on her heel and walked away, over to one of her girlfriends, Christie.

"Um, it's fine." Samantha said. "Why don't you find John and have a beer; if you're hungry there's still food out." Samantha hustled Vinny to the other side of the deck. *If I can keep these two away from each other, we should be good for the rest of the party.* Right now she had other matters to attend too, like keeping tabs on Derek and possibly getting another moment alone with him.

Throughout the rest of the evening, Samantha was busy trying to keep up with the food and cleaning. John kicked back and enjoyed their company. "There's my girl," John said proudly as Samantha came back out with the last of the desserts; chocolate-covered strawberries and some homemade cookies. When she placed them down, John gave her a little smack on her bottom and pulled her down to sit on his lap.

"John, are you sure you don't have any long lost brothers hiding out anywhere?" Samantha glance over at Lauren. She had always told Sam how much she envied her and John's relationship. She wanted what they had, at least what she thought they had.

"Nah, sorry there's only one of me; you're going to have to get in line." He got up to grab another beer. "Can I get anyone another drink? Mike, Susan... wine?"

"Oh, no man, we gotta get going. Thanks for having us, but we have an early morning."

"Right, I forgot you two are heading to Connecticut to see your aunt, right?" John grabbed another beer. Samantha was half listening; she couldn't stop peeking over at Derek on the other side of the deck. The taste of his kiss still lingered.

"Hey, did you say Manchester, Connecticut?" Derek asked, leaning up against the deck railing.

"Yep, quaint little town just outside Hartford. You ever been?" Susan replied.

"No, but I've heard of it." Derek leaned down and pulled another beer out of the cooler. "As a matter of fact, when we were moving in, I found an old bill for the old owners that was never forwarded. If I'm not mistaken, I think it was addressed to a house in Manchester, Connecticut. What are the odds? Maybe you could take it to them," Derek said, teasing.

"I doubt they want some stranger showing up at their door." Mike said.

"Do you mean the people across the street?" asked Lauren. "The people that just up and left? Weird if you ask me. The Petersons or something? Right, Sam?"

Samantha was caught off guard, she didn't want to talk about it. *Lauren, shut up for once, please.* "Patterson's. And we don't have contact with them. I guess we weren't so tight after all." Thankfully, Mike and his wife Susan were busy saying their goodbyes and John walked them out. Think quick, Sam. "Oh, Lauren, whatever happened with your blind date last weekend? I'm so sorry I meant to call you back and forgot."

"Oh forget it, he was a total weirdo. I was so creeped out, I excused myself to the ladies room and bolted out the back door of Starbucks before I even ordered my coffee." That got a little chuckle from everyone. "No one since then. I'm off dating for the moment. I am hereby declaring the summer of Lauren!" She fist pumped the air. Dramatics always worked best for her and she was making a show for Vinny, who at the moment was getting ready to leave as well. "What can I say? I am unlucky in love. I don't have the Sam touch."

"The Sam touch?" Derek stood staring at Samantha.

Shut up, Lauren, please, Samantha thought. But this sudden interest of his made her feel good. Maybe this could work in her favor.

"Oh yeah, Sam had lots of boy toys. They would fall head over heels over our little dark-haired beauty. Sam was a man-killer in college." Lauren pretended to faint.

"It wasn't that many boys, Lauren. My God, you're making me look bad!" Samantha shot her a death look. "Besides all that's ancient history. Here comes John, I'm sure he doesn't want to hear about my past conquests when we were 'on a break'. Do you, hun?"

"You ended up with me, that's all I care about." He winked at his wife then started to clean the grill while saying his good-byes with Vinny. Samantha noticed Derek staring at her with curiosity. She just waved it off as no big deal. He smiled at her.

"I'm heading out, I'll catch up with you during the week, Lauren, and it was very nice meeting you." Christie glanced at the Millers while grabbing her bag from the chair. Samantha walked her out and headed inside to clean a few things.

As Samantha walked back outside, she felt as if she walked in on some big secret. "What?"

"Nothing, I was just asking Lizzie about the baby, and I, uh, damn I'm sorry. I didn't know that they didn't know about your miscarriages."

"Oh." Samantha stopped short and looked around the table. She could feel her face beginning to flush and her stomach starting to tie in knots.

"I'm so sorry, Sam," Elizabeth said, unintentionally holding her stomach.

"It's ok. John and I are doing great, moving forward." Lauren excused herself to use the restroom before heading home; obviously she was embarrassed and upset that she had brought up something so personal to strangers. Typical Lauren. Drinks and a loose mouth. Still Sam had to forgive her. After all, she had been caught off guard with Vinny showing up. Being nervous and a little tipsy, Lauren just wasn't thinking.

"Don't think you can run for the bathroom every time you're put in the hot seat, Lau," Sam joked, letting her friend know all was forgiven. Lauren gave Samantha a kiss on the cheek and a half hug.

"I'm really sorry," she whispered in Samantha's ear.

"No worries," Samantha said and she meant it. One day she would let her new friends know, but just not today. Samantha was relieved when she noticed her husband walking towards them. *I am going to kill you later for this Vin thing, but for now thank you for saving this conversation from going any further,* she thought.

"Thanks again for inviting us over, you have lovely friends; it was nice to be surrounded by good people again. We should try to get together for dinner one night this week," Elizabeth suggested, as she and Derek were getting up to leave as well. *Boy, you talk about losing a baby and now everyone wants to leave. Great way to kill a party, Lauren.* John walked the Millers out and Samantha returned to the kitchen.

"Ok, Sam, I'm outta here." Lauren walked out of the bathroom "But first what's the scoop on your delicious new neighbor? Are they happily married?" *Here we go*, Samantha thought. "Lauren, they are expecting their first baby soon, do you think they're happy?"

"Ok, ok, don't be so sarcastic, I'm just teasing. But come on, did you see that dude's body? My Lord, I am going to need a cold shower when I get home! And maybe a little alone time."

Both girls started laughing.

"Aha, you have fun with that! Maybe you should call Vin."

"Sam…. I may be horny but I'm not desperate!"

"I am so sorry about that, I had no idea. John will hear about it later. Did you talk to him at all?"

"Are you crazy? Hell NO! I am too good for that cheat!" She flung her hair back and pushed her chest out. "Besides I was too busy chatting with Mr. Muscle from across the street. Good thing I don't live here, neighborhood watch would have a whole new meaning!"

Samantha laughed. She wanted to ask Lauren what they had talked about but she didn't want to raise any suspicions.

The two friends hugged and said goodbye. "I'll call you during the week, Lau." Lauren gave a wave as she got in her car and drove off.

Well, just in case he is looking outside his happy little home for some attention, he doesn't have to look too far, Samantha thought as she closed her front door.

CHAPTER TEN

"I thought I'd find you sitting out here; safe to come sit?"

"Hey, stranger, as safe as ever. Want one?" Sam held up her mug for Derek to see.

"Sure."

Samantha came back handing him a steaming cup of coffee. "Milk, no sugar, I didn't forget," she joked.

"Mmm, freshly brewed coffee, I almost forgot how good it is. I've been working so much lately I've been running on coffee that's been sitting in the pot all day. This is good, just what I need. "

"Is this what we're going to chat about now? How good my coffee is?" Samantha giggled.

Derek looked confused and a little ashamed.

"So?" she persisted.

"So…" Derek paused and then laughed. There was another brief silence.

"I guess I just wanted to clear the air," he said. "Are we ok? I mean, I don't know what came over me at the barbeque. To be honest I was almost afraid to walk over here."

"Dead man walking," Samantha teased holding her hands out in front of her as if they were in handcuffs. "We're good, don't worry about it." She laughed. "It was a moment. Maybe not the best timing but all it was, was a moment. A kiss. Obviously there is an attraction between us and maybe we just needed to get it out of the way." Finally, after what felt like an eternity, Derek responded.

"For what is worth, you're an excellent kisser," he said with a smirk, showing off his sexy dimple again.

"Well thanks, you're not so bad yourself."

"Oh, I know." They both laughed.

"Seriously though, Sam, it can't happen again. I mean what about John and Lizzie….my god, Lizzie is carrying my son."

"Derek, don't worry about it. It was a one-time incident that came out of left field. Believe me, you won't find a rabbit boiling on your stove. I'm not Glenn Close and this isn't 'Fatal Attraction.'

"Do you feel guilty about it?"

Now was the time to let him know how she felt. She didn't want to scare him off, but she didn't want him to think she was so loose with her lips with every guy she met.

"Honestly?" *Ok, don't blow this, girl.* "Not really. Don't get me wrong, I love John, but, I don't know, when you're with the same person for so long…sometimes you lose that passion. I can't lie. It was kind of nice to kiss another man. You know…"

"The excitement of it all," they both said out loud.

"I know." He sighed. "It's been so long for me as well. Look, I don't want to make excuses, but since the move Lizzie has been working a lot, and not to sound like a complete prick, but her hormones are crazy and she is about to have a baby. I sound like a tool, huh? A real winner of a husband."

"Stop. Please. I was just as into it as you. Please don't feel guilty. And no, you sound like a normal man to me, one with a pulse." *Please, don't stop now* she thought, *I'm just getting started.*

"Thanks, Sam. Let's face it, you and I have been spending a lot of time together. We understand each other. After all, we have very similar situations with our home lives. We have MIA spouses that leave us alone to fend for ourselves." He was smiling.

"So, it's their fault!" At least now he was smiling again and once again being a little flirty. "Seriously, Derek, I really don't want there to be any weirdness between us. I enjoy our time together. Honestly, it's not a big deal and I'm cool with it. I'm not looking for us to run off together." Samantha chuckled.

"No? Gee, here I was thinking a kiss from me would have sent you home to pack! I must be losing my touch!" He laughed.

"Aren't you so full of yourself? I think it's more a case that you just can't resist my beauty! Admit it, Mr. Miller, you want it!"

He looked at her and smiled. Not an innocent smile. A very seductive smile.

That one little smile was all Samantha needed.

CHAPTER ELEVEN

"What a beautiful night." Elizabeth announced as she and her husband sat on the Bennett's front wraparound porch with them. "Derek, we must get one of these porch swings, it's so relaxing."

Samantha stood there in her tight maxi dress with a plunging neckline and slit that went on for days. One thing for sure Samantha Bennett had all the right things in all the right places and she knew it. Standing with confidence she noticed Derek's eyes on her and could sense Elizabeth's frustration with her husband waiting for an answer.

Elizabeth shifted on the swing, drawing Derek's attention towards her. She cleared her throat. "What do you think, hun?"

Samantha watched as Derek looked over at his wife and rubbed his hand down her thigh. "What was that? You like this swing?" Elizabeth just stared back at him and nodded. She took his hand and placed it on her belly, Samantha could feel that

Elizabeth was playing up the baby card for her benefit. Always acting like such a confident woman she was surprised to see Elizabeth be so territorial. Who knew Elizabeth was insecure, obviously Samantha's presence was overshadowing Elizabeth. It was apparent Elizabeth was making it known that this was her territory when she placed her hand over his while Derek rubbed her belly and smiled at him. Derek smiled back at his wife which only made Samantha take charge of the conversation once again.

"Oh, I love the swing. I sit out here all the time. It really is peaceful." Samantha had noticed Derek petting his wife's belly and felt a sting of jealousy. Although, she had also noticed him glancing at her quite a few times. A few of those times their eyes had locked, Samantha making sure she was the first to look away. But even while rubbing his wife's belly she noticed Derek watching her every move. And she wasn't complaining. She enjoyed knowing that this handsome man was stealing glances at her and was barely acknowledging his wife. Feeling empowered, Samantha made sure to command the attention of the group. She would cross her legs in Derek's direction to get his attention or run her fingers through her hair to show her neck; all little motions made to ensure that her neighbor had his eye on her. And it worked.

John was too preoccupied with his phone to notice. No matter where they were or what they were doing, it was always in his hands. Once he put his phone down he stood up and grabbed his empty beer bottle. "Can I grab you another beer, man?"

"Sure, thanks!" Derek lifted up his empty for John to take in. John shuffled back into the house whistling an old Def Leppard tune which made the group laugh. "What?" John asked, looking back puzzled.

Samantha hopped up and started to sing. "Pour some sugar on me…" She swayed back and forth, grabbing everyone's attention. John shook his head laughing and went inside.

"Come on and fire me up!" Derek chimed in.

Samantha stood there giggling, looking at Derek. She wondered if he thought about their first kiss as much as she did. Just as she was going to sing the next line, Elizabeth spoke.

"We really had a great time at the barbeque, you have great friends. I really liked Lauren, she was fun."

Samantha couldn't help but notice the woman becoming increasingly uncomfortable. Elizabeth shifted on the swing to stretch her back and neck

As if Derek knew Elizabeth needed reassurance, he reached over and rubbed his wife's back.

Samantha watched with envy the way his hands touched his wife with careful strokes. She couldn't help but remember what it felt like to have his hands on her, the taste of his kiss. Watching him only made her want him more, he was hot and that one kiss had awoken something up inside of Samantha. However, they had both agreed it couldn't happen again. Right?

John reappeared with the beers and handed one to Derek. As he sat down, Samantha noticed John was holding something.

It's show time!

"Hey, Sam, did you ask Derek if he wanted the tickets yet?" John leaned over and placed two ballgame tickets in Derek's hand.

"Oh, I forgot…"

"No way, this is next week's game. You're offering me tickets to see the Rays vs. Yankees? How much?" He looked like a kid in the candy store.

"Yes, they are all yours, free of charge," said Sam. "Just so happens that one of Lauren's customers gave them to her, but she's not a sports fan at all. She knows John and I like to go every now and then, but of course my husband has to work so…" Samantha let her words trail off again. She sat there smiling, confident that this would end in her favor. She caught a glimpse of Elizabeth who looked confused. She could tell she was on the verge of saying something.

"When I spoke with Elizabeth the other day, she mentioned that you would've loved to go to a game. I just happened to come into some tickets." Samantha shrugged her shoulders. *And as long as I keep you from mentioning this to Lauren, if you should see her, I am golden.*

"This is awesome, Lizzie, do you think you can get off work?" Derek looked back at his wife.

"Derek, I don't think so… it's too short notice and honestly I don't know if I'm up to it."

"Yeah, it was a long shot, you're right, you would be so uncomfortable in those seats." Derek hung his head down looking at the tickets one last time before passing them back to John. He looked like he'd lost his best friend.

Samantha saw guilt come across Elizabeth's face and was pleased with her reaction. *There is no way she would deny her husband a night out and how could she hold him back from going. Elizabeth would never want to be the bad guy,* Samantha thought.

"Hey, there are two perfectly good tickets here, great seats, why not go with Samantha? She enjoys the game more than I do at times."

Thank you, John, you are making this way too easy for me.

Derek and Samantha looked over at Elizabeth, waiting for her approval. She shifted uncomfortably in her seat. Samantha sat quietly while she waited for Elizabeth to answer. She didn't want to push the issue and give Elizabeth the wrong idea.

"If you have to work Lizzie, and Sam doesn't mind putting up with me at the game for a night, would you mind? I mean, I would hate for the tickets to go to waste."

"Sure, go, sounds like fun! You guys will have a great time. That's very sweet of you to offer the tickets. I'm sure Derek will have more fun with you then me anyway; I'm not much of a sports fan!"

Derek's face lit up like the Rockefeller Center's Christmas tree.

Once inside their house, Elizabeth kept replaying the scene on the Bennett's porch over and over in her mind. She was confused with what had just taken place. For starters, why was Samantha parading around, dancing like she belonged on a pole in front of them? Was she inadvertently trying to seduce Derek, her husband? Or was Elizabeth just feeling insecure and insignificant? Being pregnant is a beautiful thing and Derek reassured her almost daily on her beauty, but she felt like a beached whale. Elizabeth never felt inferior to other women, she had a confidence that men were drawn too. So why is she feeling this way? She knew deep down she was just as pretty as Samantha but the image of her shaking her ass in front of her husband just made Lizzie mad.

The tickets, that's what really was bothering Elizabeth. She was positive that she had just had this conversation about the tickets to Samantha. Is this all too coincidental? Surely Samantha was just being neighborly, right? After all this was her friend. Why should she feel threatened by a silly baseball game with hundreds of people around them? What could happen? Oh, Lizzie, stop being so naïve, they are going in the car alone for an hour. Anything can happen. Stop, Lizzie. You are letting your hormones get to you. There is nothing to be worried about. But still something was so off with this whole thing. She couldn't put her finger on it but something was off with her new neighbor.

"Lizzie, how awesome is this? I'm excited to finally see a Rays-Yankees game *in* Yankee Stadium!! That was so generous of them to think of me, it's a good thing Lauren didn't want the tickets." Derek rambled on about the game as he changed.

Yeah, real generous and convenient, my God if I have to listen to him go on and on about those tickets I am going to explode. Hmmm… is it the game he is excited about or going with little

Mrs. Perfect Figure? I need to say something. And she wanted to; but instead she just nodded.

She looked at her reflection in the master bathroom mirror and didn't like this weight on her shoulders. It was eating away at her and she knew she shouldn't feel this way, but it bothered her. It actually bothered her that out of nowhere Samantha had come across these tickets and offered them to her husband. She had just had this conversation with Samantha and she knew she wouldn't be able to take the time off nor did she really want to. On the other hand this was her friend. They confided with one another and had started to become real friends. Sam wouldn't purposely buy tickets just to spend time with Derek, right? After all they saw each other all the time while she and John are at work. But that sinking feeling in the pit of her stomach resurfaced. She took a deep breath and looked in the mirror once more and pulled her hair out of its ponytail.

"It's awesome," Elizabeth pulled back the sheets on their bed. *Since no one else seems to think it's really not appropriate for my husband to go out with the neighborhood trophy wife, I have no choice but to think that this is just so awesome. Peachy fucking keen! Who in their right mind lets their husband go out with another woman? Who? ME! That's who, you idiot.*

"Are you sure you don't mind?" Derek asked, breaking her from her thoughts. He stood there in the bathroom doorway holding his toothbrush looking like he had won his first Pulitzer. His expression was so light-hearted, he was beaming with excitement. How could I say no to him? Elizabeth thought.

"It's fine, Derek, really. I just…I don't know." She walked over to the bathroom doorway letting out a big sigh and watched as Derek finished brushing his teeth. She knew she had to get this off her chest. Maybe saying something to him would make her feel better, more secure with the situation. Or maybe she would be picking a fight that she wasn't in the mood for. Either way she needed to say something; most sane women wouldn't even allow their husband near another female. *I'm practically handing mine over!*

"Derek, I'm happy that you get to go to the game. Really, I am. But there's something bothering me about these tickets. And before you get upset with me, please hear me out. When Sam was over here helping me unpack the kitchen, I mentioned how I wanted to do something special for you. Buying baseball tickets was that something special. I didn't think I could get off work, but to be honest, I just didn't feel like sitting in the sun, being pregnant and watching a game I could care less about. Derek, Sam knew this. Don't you think that's a little odd? A little, I don't know, coincidental?"

He dropped his toothbrush on the counter and walked over to his wife. He wrapped his arms around her expanding waist and kissed her forehead. "Oh, Lizzie, do I detect a hint of jealousy? You know you have nothing to worry about. I'm going to be so into the game I'll barely notice who's with me."

Sure, because bombshell Sam is so easy to ignore!

"She said Lauren had the tickets and didn't want them…does it really matter where they came from? I get to go; wasn't that what you wanted in the first place?" Derek couldn't hide his excitement.

Elizabeth wanted him to understand and sympathize with her and agree to not go. She wanted to tell him, no, you can't go. But she knew she was defeated. She also knew that she had to trust her husband. After all, it was only a baseball game. Reluctantly she hugged him and kissed his cheek. "Well, as long as the players are the only ones making home runs and not you, I guess I shouldn't rain on your parade. You're right, I'm glad you can go. Have fun."

Derek laughed and kissed his wife goodnight.

Elizabeth tossed and turned in bed, she couldn't get comfortable. *Nothing you can do now, the damage is done. Push it aside, it's only a game. Still, Lizzie, are you jealous of your husband spending time with another woman or are you just jealous of Samantha? Shit! face it Lizzie, you're jealous of your friend.*

"Can you blame me?" she whispered to herself.

CHAPTER TWELVE

It was game day! Samantha had counted down the days until she and Derek would be alone at last. Getting to spend the whole day with Derek alone and not having to share him except for the thousands of fans at Yankee Stadium was thrilling. She had even bought herself a Yankee Jersey with Jeter's name, a navy blue tank for underneath to match and a pair of denim shorts paired up with some wedge sandals. Samantha primped and fixed her hair all morning long waiting impatiently for her 'date' to arrive. She was all set.

They had planned on leaving earlier in the afternoon, hopefully avoiding the traffic into the Bronx. Derek suggested tailgating with all the other fans, but Samantha insisted on just grabbing some beers and hot dogs during the game. Derek said that Elizabeth would have never eaten a hot dog from the stadium let alone be the one to suggest it. Samantha smiled to herself, score one for me.

Once she heard a knock on the front door, the butterflies in her stomach started stirring. With one last peek in the mirror, she grabbed her bag from her bed and headed downstairs.

"Hey!" Samantha greeted Derek with a sweet smile and a kiss on the cheek. From one simple peck on the cheek Samantha's heart raced. Impure thoughts surfaced to the front of her mind, making her giddy. Hoping he wouldn't see what an effect he had on her, she quickly turned to lock the front door in order to hide that she was blushing. *Mr. Miller, what you do to me.... you always look so good and smell divine!*

He stepped back, giving her room to lock the door. "Ready? Let's roll!" Samantha said turning, making sure she added a little pep to her step. She pranced down the walkway to the car with Derek in tow. Samantha knew Derek was watching her every move, she glanced over her shoulder and caught him checking out her ass.

Derek opened the car door for her. "I'm pumped! I can't thank you enough for thinking of me."

Samantha knew Derek was watching her as she climbed up into his Dodge Ram. *How could he not, I look hot!*

Samantha smiled and watched as he walked around the front of his truck and hopped into the driver's seat. Derek started the engine and the radio blasted some tune loud enough to make them both jump. Samantha put her hand to her chest laughing.

"My god, you almost gave me a heart attack. Do you always listen to your music this loud?"

"Sorry, I didn't realize I had it turned up," Derek chuckled, feeling slightly embarrassed while turning the radio off.

"And wait, was that country?" she asked. "Mr. Miller, are you listening to country music? Or am I going deaf now thanks to your lack of volume control?"

"And if it is country, wise ass?"

"Wise ass, huh? You're starting a little early with the compliments, I see. Last I recall you enjoyed touching this wise ass."

Derek cleared his throat and went on, ignoring her flirtatious comment. "Anyway, Zac Brown band, ever hear of them?" Derek turned the radio on low.

"Yes, I have. I like some country, believe it or not, but I'm more of a dance music kind of girl. I like to shake my groove thang." Sam laughed out loud, snapping her fingers and dancing in her seat.

"Really? Your groove thang, huh? Looks more like you're having a fit as opposed to dancing!"

"I could stop then if you like." Samantha crossed her arms around her chest, looking all serious.

"Oh, I wouldn't want you to stop shaking anything, Sam. Please, by all means shake away!"

"Can't really get my groove on with this little ditty on, but I'll let you listen to your music."

"Ok, ok, I get the hint. Dance music it is." Derek turned the station. "I would have never pegged you as someone who listened to any country. Pop, yes, country, not so much."

"Why's that?"

"Oh, I don't know, you just don't strike me as the country music type, that's all." He looked down at Samantha's newly manicured fingernails and pedicure.

Samantha followed his gaze and concluded that he was most likely sizing her up as being high maintenance. All it took for most people was one look to assume that she was a spoiled rich brat, which always made her laugh. What, a girl can't have style? Samantha had learned to shrug the opinions of others aside; she was always misjudged and underestimated. Which deep down suited her just fine, for Samantha was always full of surprises.

"I know what you're thinking, Derek. I know you look at me and think there's a woman with everything. Designer shoes, manicured nails, nice car; there must not be much going on upstairs. Well, you know, looks can be deceiving. I am as intelligent as I am feisty and I always get what I want."

"Oh, do you?"

"Hmmm, you wait Mr. Miller, I just might surprise you one of these days." She batted her long lashes.

"You do surprise me, every time we have our friendly little chats I peel back another layer of Sam!" Derek laughed.

He muttered under his breath, "As much as I fight it, I can't help but want to keep digging at those layers!"

"What's that?" Samantha looked over at Derek.

"Oh, nothing." Derek smiled.

"These seats are incredible, right behind third base. Sam, I have been to more stadiums than I can remember, but being here is just awesome. I can't believe Lauren just gave you these tickets. She's crazy!"

"That's Lauren, crazy." Aside from Derek ignoring Samantha's flirtatious comments the rest of the ride to the game had been amazing. They had laughed, sang and told corny jokes. It felt natural, not forced. They enjoyed each other's company. It wasn't only a physical attraction, they had a real connection. So maybe it was time she came clean about a couple of things.

"Well, if you want to know the truth."

"Uh oh, the truth? This sounds interesting. Is there something you would like to share with the rest of the class, Mrs. Bennett?"

"Yes, the truth. I'm not sure you're ready for it."

"I'm ready for anything you can dish out, Mrs. Bennett."

"Well, then here it goes. I think Lauren may have a little crush on you."

"Me? You're kidding."

"Yeah, you. Can't say I blame her. You are a very nice-looking guy. And don't act like you don't know it." Sam rolled her eyes and shrugged his comment off.

"I'm just your average-looking man, nothing special here. I think Lauren needs to adjust her standards a little higher. But tell her thanks."

"Thanks?"

"Yeah, thanks. For if it wasn't for her so-called crush, you would never had said that I'm good-looking. It's not every day a married guy gets a compliment from a hot chick." Derek was teasing but his eyes said something else. If Samantha wasn't mistaken, this gorgeous man sitting next to her wasn't conceited; if anything she detected some low self-esteem.

Well, I can fix that.

"Oh, whatever, Mr. Miller, you know you got it. You certainly don't need me to tell you that. And don't act like you don't know you're the talk of the neighborhood. And as for calling you good-looking, yes you are. You are more than handsome; you are extremely intelligent and fun to be around. You are not only eye candy, you are a passionate man. Hmm, I guess we are both misjudged people, another thing in common. So there." She punched his arm gently and smiled at him.

"Ok, ok. You don't have to beat me up." Derek laughed and grabbed her hand, they looked up at one another and smiled. He reluctantly took his hand from hers and went to grab his wallet, looking for the beer guy.

"Still, I guess Lauren's shit out of luck," Samantha said. "Lucky me, I get to sit here with you."

"I beg to differ, I'm the lucky one," Derek said.

They smiled shyly. After a couple of minutes of silence Samantha said, "Well, let's not upset the poor girl and let her know we went together. Maybe we should keep it our little secret."

"Sure, what's another secret?" He laughed, feeling a little uncomfortable keeping another secret from his wife.

"So, did Lizzie go to games with you back home?"

"Well, she's been to a couple, but mostly it was me and a few buddies of mine or my dad. Lizzie doesn't really share in my love of sports." Derek was scanning the outfield, watching the players warm up.

"I'm surprised. It was part of your job, and you love the game. I know I would want to go with my husband, show him my support, but I also lived in a house with my uncle who was a Yankee fanatic; I grew up going to games."

Derek turned to face her, smiling. "Well, Samantha, I am happy to be here with you now and it's going to be a great game when my Tampa Bay Rays kick your New York Yankee ass!"

"One can dream!" They both laughed and watched as the game started.

Samantha couldn't believe how this had all worked out, how she'd been able to manipulate the situation to get her way. Maybe it was the excitement of something new. How could a simple baseball game make her this happy? At first she had thought they just had chemistry, now she realized they had a real connection. Samantha hadn't felt this way in a while. She wanted this man sitting next to her, but she also knew she needed to keep her feelings at bay. *Still, he does look hot in his Rays Jersey! How am I going to stop myself? A little dabble won't hurt. Famous last words.*

During the innings, Derek grabbed a few beers and a hot dog for each of them. They ate and laughed and were having a really great time. The couple sitting next to them were fellow Yankee fans, and they joined in on the fun as well. When the stadium did the wave, Samantha and Derek stood up and raised their hands together, standing so close to one another she could feel his body heat.

When the concession guy came around with beer, neither Samantha nor Derek corrected the man next to them when he asked Derek if his wife wanted another one. Samantha could barely contain her satisfaction. Other people thought they were a couple; they not only acted like a couple but they looked like one as well. Samantha basked in the notion that they really had something between them. *Well, John told me to make a fresh start, no one said where I should look.*

Derek leaned back in his seat lifting his ankle to rest over his knee. Thoughts raced through his mind whenever he caught a glance of Samantha. Here he was with his sexy-as-hell neighbor, who not only looked good in a baseball jersey, but knew the game. He watched as she cheered on the Yankees for scoring a run. Every moment spent with her, he was more and more smitten. He swung his arm around the back of Samantha's chair. He gently pulled on a strand of her hair causing her to look in the opposite direction. She looked back, assuming her hair was stuck in the seat. After he pulled on her hair for a second time, she chuckled and slapped his arm. Derek tried to play it off as if he didn't know what had happened.

Their gaze always held longer than it probably should have. And with each innocent touch of a hand or stolen glance, they both felt the same spark. Samantha knew this man wanted her just as much as she wanted him, but she also knew it wouldn't be easy. Derek was a good man and wouldn't fall into bed with just anyone. Cheating was not on his agenda, but in true Samantha style, she knew how to get what she wanted, by any means necessary.

Thinking to herself about how this man would most likely never cheat on his wife, she fought the urge to reach over and kiss him. Samantha wanted to take his face into her hands, run her fingers over his dimple and look into his captivating blue eyes and just kiss him. She bit her bottom lip, remembering Derek's kiss. If only there was a way. Her thoughts were interrupted when Derek jumped up and shielded her from a flying ball.

Out of the corner of his eye he had seen the ball flying straight for them. The ball came crashing down into the empty seat in the row behind them, just missing Samantha's head. The ball bounced and dropped and then began to roll under their seats; Derek leaned down and was able to grab hold of it before it continued to roll. He sat up and raised his arm to show the captured ball. The crowd roared in excitement.

"Oh geez, thank god you saw that coming." Samantha raised her hands to the top of her head. "I would not have enjoyed a night in the emergency room with a concussion."

"Stick with me and you'll be alright, kid!" Derek winked. He tossed the ball back and forth from hand to hand as he watched the game and scanned the crowd. A minute later he excused himself.

Samantha watched as Derek strode a few rows ahead; there was a little boy of about seven years old wearing a Yankee t-shirt and hat, sitting with his father. She saw Derek bend down in the aisle and chat with the boy. Derek handed over the ball and patted the kid on his back.

When Derek returned to his seat, Samantha looked over and saw him grinning. "I noticed that boy with his father watching me after I caught the ball. He looked a little disappointed that he didn't catch it, he had his mitt ready, just waiting too." He shrugged and gave Samantha a wink.

"You, Mr. Miller, will be a great father."

"I hope so. I had a good role model so if I'm half as good as my old man, my little guy will be lucky. I appreciate the vote of confidence, it means a lot. I'm excited, won't be long until he's here." Derek paused and continued to watch the game. "People always say that once your baby is born and you hold them for the very first time - ah, shit, I'm sorry Sam." Derek shook his head and put his arm on the back of her chair. "Here I am running my mouth…" his words trailed off as Samantha leaned back and rested her head on his shoulder.

"It's ok, Derek." Samantha spoke softly. "I'm happy for you, no worries. I'm ok. Like I said, you will be a great dad." She looked up at him and gave a sheepish grin, trying to cover up her pain.

"You really are amazing Sam. Here I am, rambling like an ass about my baby and you manage to hide your pain and be supportive. I am so sorry about your loss. I don't know what to say, but I'm here for you. You can talk to me. I've wanted to ask ever since Lauren mentioned it at the barbeque, but I didn't want to pry, it's none of my business. I'm sure John is being supportive. It's not my place, but I'm here for you."

"Thank you, Derek. There's not much to tell, I miscarried… twice. I'm not sure babies are in my future. John and I are moving forward and we'll see where it takes us. I appreciate your support. Lord knows I haven't had much of it lately." Samantha sat up, gripping the edge of the seat with both hands, staring off into the distance. Derek leaned forward as well, lacing his fingers together, resting his elbows on his thighs. He looked over and stared at Samantha. When she finally looked his way he noticed a single tear sliding down her cheek.

CHAPTER THIRTEEN

"Derek, we didn't have to leave, the game's not even over. Don't you want to see the Yankees win?" Samantha teased as she leaned up on the side of Derek's truck in the stadium parking lot. She didn't want her misfortune to ruin their evening.

"Sam, I loved being at the game; it was fun especially with you, but you're upset. I think that's a little more important than who wins." He rested on his truck next to her, crossing his arms in front of his chest. "Talk to me."

Although she had ulterior motives for this evening, Samantha did need someone to talk to. She wasn't made of stone and lately John had been so preoccupied with work she needed a release. Samantha took a deep breath in and let it out slowly.

"It took John and me years to get pregnant. I was starting to lose hope, and we actually had gone to the doctor to discuss other options. A few days later I realized that I was already pregnant. I can't even begin to tell you how elated we were. I quit my job at the accounting office so I could stay at home and start to prepare. I know people thought I was crazy for quitting work so soon, but I was excited. I wanted everything to be perfect and enjoy the pregnancy without having the stress of work. I went for my first sonogram appointment; I was about eight weeks. I didn't know what was going on. The stenographer was hitting buttons on the keyboard, trying to capture a better view and that's when I noticed a look of worry on her face. When she excused herself, I knew something was wrong…there was no heartbeat. We were devastated; it took some time for us to move forward. I mean, it had taken so long and within just a few short weeks, it had all ended. I never returned to work. John suggested I take the time to get back on my feet and rest."

Samantha paused and looked at Derek for a minute before continuing. "Honestly, we weren't even trying again and I got pregnant within a few months. This time around it happened so quickly, I was shocked. I was afraid though, I didn't want to do anything, I was afraid of miscarrying again, but I survived the first trimester. I was feeling more confident. We started to buy things for the nursery; miscarriages after the first trimester rarely happen. I was close to the end of my second when I went into early labor. It was a girl…Alexa Jane."

Samantha wiped away the tears that had begun to stream down her face. She looked at Derek who was staring at her with compassion. She forced a weak smile.

"Jane was my mother's name." Holding back her tears she continued. "The doctors suggested we go for therapy, which we did. But after a few sessions John didn't go with me anymore.

He felt he was over it and that I should put it behind me. Soon he was repeating the shrink's advice; I should make a fresh start. I stopped opening up about my feelings to him. I know he cares, I just think he ran out of patience with me. I don't know anymore." There was a long pause…"oh, Derek, It was horrible." The tears became harder. She turned and fell into his open arms. He held her while she wept, rubbing her back and kissing the top of her head. He wished there was something he could do.

"Sam, I'm so sorry." He continued to rub his hands up and down her back until the crying subsided. She looked up at Derek and he wiped away the last of her tears with his thumbs. His heart ached for her; he couldn't imagine what it felt like to go through that not once, but twice. He wanted to take the pain away. He wanted her to feel safe.

He thought John was more supportive, but he was wrong. He should have known. Whenever they all were together, John always had his phone, whether it was talking, texting, or emailing. That guy paid more attention to his cell than his wife. Derek liked John, they were buddies. But it bothered Derek that John had this beautiful woman who loved and adored him and he neglected her, especially when she needed him most. Derek, normally a very easy going guy, didn't care for John's nonchalant attitude towards his wife, who obviously needed emotional support. Derek knew it wasn't his place to get involved but he also knew what it was like to not have the support you needed. After all, his own wife didn't seem to show interest in anything that he wanted or needed these days. And now that Samantha had confirmed his suspicions, he wanted to be there for her. Maybe they could be there for each other. It was almost as if they were lost souls.

At least that's what he thought.

"I'm sorry; I don't know what came over me." Samantha leaned in and rested her forehead on Derek's chest.

"Shh, don't be silly, we're friends, Sam, and I'm here anytime you need me."

Samantha looked up and met his eyes; they stood frozen in time, both their hearts started to pound. She could feel the chemistry between them growing, both wanting to touch the other. This man was a godsend, he was hot, sensitive and he was going to give her what she needed, what she craved. But this was getting too deep too quick, she never opened up with anyone the way she just had with Derek. Samantha wanted to lighten the mood.

She leaned up on her toes until she was almost face to face with Derek. She could smell his sweet breath. She licked her bottom lip. "I think my Yankees kicked your Tampa Bay ass!"

Derek was confused for a moment, then heard the crowd cheering as they exited the stadium, chanting "YANKEES, YANKEES!"

He couldn't help but throw his head back, laughing. Between consoling Samantha and fighting the urge to grab and kiss her, he hadn't noticed the fans leaving the ballpark.

"Are you ready, smartass?" Derek chuckled as he opened the truck door for Samantha.

She turned around to face him before hopping up into the seat. "Thank you, Derek, for a fun night out, and for listening to me. I'm sure this wasn't what you had in mind when I offered you ballgame tickets."

"Sam, it was a perfect night." He smiled, showcasing his sweet dimple.

Samantha's feelings were growing stronger and she thought Derek felt the same, but she felt he was holding back. "That dimple is adorable." She gently stroked his cheek sliding her finger over the indent. *Come on, Derek, you know you want it… come on boy, kiss me, kiss me now.*

Derek reached up, placing his hand over Samantha's; "Sam… we should go before we do something that we'll regret."

"No regrets here!" Samantha leaned up and kissed him.

She had wanted him to make the first move, hell she wasn't sure how much more fishing she would have to do before he took the bait, but she couldn't fight the urge any longer.

She wrapped her hands around Derek's neck while he moved one of his arms around her waist. Derek jumped into the passenger seat with Samantha and pulled her on his lap to straddle him. Within minutes the windows were fogged up. Their breathing became heavier and faster. Derek unbuttoned Samantha's jersey and helped her take it off. Her breasts were so full, pushing out from the top of her tank. Derek leaned in, grabbing her breast with both hands, and pressed his lips to her porcelain skin. Her skin was so soft and smelled like warm vanilla sugar. It reminded him of their first kiss in her pantry closet. He hadn't stopped thinking about it since.

He lost all sense of control. Samantha lifted his chin and pressed her lips against his; he parted his mouth, allowing their tongues to slide in and out.

"Derek, you are driving me crazy."

"I want you, Samantha, I do, but… I'm sorry, I just…this is getting too heavy for me." He looked away.

Samantha sat stunned for a minute, trying to understand what had just happened. Her breathing began to steady and she looked at Derek.

"Derek, what's wrong? I thought you were enjoying it…I certainly was!"

"I know, I am, I mean I was…"

"So what's wrong?"

"Sam, I don't know what's going on, all the time we've spent together, that first kiss….I don't know, it's like I'm hypnotized by you. I look into your big green eyes and I lose all sense of control. They're captivating. You're sexy as hell and I would be lying if I said I didn't want more, but it has to stop here."

"Derek, we had this conversation before, remember?

"I know, but we really need to get a better hold on this. We're not kids anymore and we're both married.

"I understand that we are both married, but you can't deny this thing we share." Samantha grabbed her jersey and began to dress. "I guess you're right though. We should stop, but you can't tell me you don't feel the same."

"Doesn't matter what we feel, nothing can ever come from it. I should take you home." With that Derek got out of the truck to switch seats.

CHAPTER FOURTEEN

A few days had gone by since the ball game and Samantha hadn't seen or heard from Derek. She sent emails and texts, but he never responded. She hoped she hadn't scared him off. Samantha had never had any trouble before 'getting the guy' so she couldn't understand why Derek always pulled back. They were both married, but she sensed there was something more. She would back off and give him space. She was used to getting her way, but she didn't want to push him away completely. Samantha was about to make a pot of coffee when she heard the doorbell ring.

"Oh, hi!" Samantha greeted the mailman as she took the pile of mail along with a package that was too big for the mailbox. "Thank you!"

Samantha sorted through the envelopes, and came across one addressed to her. She tore open the paper and pulled out an invitation for a baby shower. Immediately her heart sank. She stood there with the invitation in her hand and felt her body start to tremble. All she could think was, she didn't get to have a shower. When would she get to have her baby? The last thing she wanted to do was put a smile on her face and go to some other woman's baby shower. The thought of having to go to the store and buy a gift made her light-headed. Samantha took in deep breaths and calmed herself down. She hoped this was an event she could miss, maybe this was for someone that she could blow off and say she and John would be out of town. With some hope she opened the card to see who it was from.

John's partner's wife was expecting. How could she have forgotten that? *Why am I being invited to this shower?* Samantha knew Scott and his wife Jennifer, but they barely spoke. She only saw them once a year at the firm's holiday party or if someone hosted a party at their house, which was rare. Samantha picked up the telephone and dialed.

"John Bennett"

"Hey, sorry to bother you, but did you know I was being invited to Jen's shower?"

"Yes, Scott mentioned it the other day."

"So, you didn't think to mention it to me? I barely speak to the woman; what makes you think I would go, John?"

"Why, wouldn't you go Sam? I think it's nice she included you. You're my wife and I work with Scott; it's out of respect for me that you were invited."

"John, have you forgotten so quickly? Don't you think this would be hard for me? How can I go and pretend like nothing happened? They all know, John. They know what we've been through. They're all going to stare and talk behind my back or pretend like they care and ask me how I'm doing." Samantha tried to hide the hurt in her voice and choked back a sob.

"Sam, I really don't want to have this discussion again. First off, what makes you think they don't care? How would you know? You don't exactly make yourself available to these women. How many times did Jennifer invite you to lunch? How many times did you cancel saying you're too busy? Jesus, Sam, you're acting like a child. Other women are allowed to have babies. I'm sorry, Samantha, but you will have to learn to accept that. Are you saying you can't be happy for someone else?"

"Wait, what? No, that's not it at all. I know that other woman are allowed to get pregnant, but I'm your wife. You can be so insensitive to how I feel sometimes. And please do not say, find a fresh start. That's the last thing I want to hear. I just –it's still very new, the wounds have not healed. I don't think they ever will and I …" Her words trailed off as John began to speak.

"Samantha, you don't want to go, that's fine. You know how I feel about this topic. I'm sorry, I don't want to be an insensitive prick, but it's time to move forward. Listen, I have to go, I'll see you later."

Samantha stood frozen with disbelief. How could John act so coldly? He didn't understand or know how hard it was to go on Facebook and see how someone else was pregnant with their next baby. She was tired of seeing everyone else's sonogram photos being posted on their pages. It took everything she had to press the 'like' button or leave a comment congratulating them. Everywhere she turned there was something that reminded her of her loss, just the sight of baby clothing, or the Gerber commercials could bring her to tears. The pain was still there, time didn't heal all wounds. Now being invited to Jen's shower was the last thing she needed; she wasn't strong enough to put on a happy face and sit with all these other women who she knew didn't care if she was there or not. Before Samantha experienced her own two miscarriages, she felt sorry for women who had lost pregnancies but had never fully understood the devastation until now.

Samantha paced back and forth through the kitchen and living room. Her body was shaking as the tears streamed down her face. No one understood what it was like. She couldn't confide in her own husband anymore about her biggest loss, their biggest loss. She was alone, she was always alone and this was one battle she had to fight on her own. It was times like this that she wished her mother were alive. She had always known the right thing to say to make her feel better.

Samantha placed the phone back on the charger and heard a knock on the door. She tried wiping the tears from her face and looked in the foyer mirror before opening the door. *Great, my face is a hot mess! Who's here now?*

"Hey, Sam."

"Derek, what are you doing here?"

"Can I come in for a minute?" Derek stood on the front porch with his hands in his pockets. He looked good in his denim shorts and blue t-shirt, but Samantha had the feeling it wasn't a friendly visit.

She stepped back allowing Derek to enter. She tried to steal a glimpse of herself in the mirror again. Just as she suspected, her eyes were still swollen and red. They made their way into the kitchen and Samantha hit the start button on the coffee maker. "Do you want a cup of coffee?"

"Sure…Sam, I just wanted to come by and apologize."

"No, Derek, I'm the one who needs to apologize. My behavior lately is inexcusable and I'm sorry for the other night. I shouldn't have dumped all that on you."

"Wait, Sam, what's wrong? Have you been crying?" Derek took a step closer and rested his hand on her shoulder.

"Oh, it's alright, I'm fine, really." Samantha grabbed the milk and sugar and placed them on the table along with two mugs.

"Sam…"

Samantha let out a sigh as she grabbed the invitation off the counter and handed it to Derek. He read the invitation and looked over at Samantha. "So, you feel like salt was thrown on an open wound, huh?"

"Silly, right? You can say it, everyone else does."

"I don't think it's silly, I think you have every right to feel upset. Sam, what you experienced was unimaginable. Whether it's been a few months or years, doesn't mean you're not allowed to feel the pain."

Samantha was shocked; did Derek really understand her? Her own husband couldn't understand why she couldn't move forward and forget what happened. He had made peace with the situation and that meant she should to, but she just couldn't let it go. She sat down after filling both mugs with coffee. Derek placed the invite back on the counter and took the seat across from her.

"Ya know, I know people think I have it easy staying at home while John works, and for the most part it is, but it's not all it's cracked up to be. I don't just sit on my ass all day, and it does get lonely. I've gotten used to the fact that I come second to John's work. I've actually grown to just accept it, but I thought having a family would help. Maybe even bring us closer like when we were first married. When we lost our baby…John drowned himself in work and I started to question everything. What did I do? What could I have done differently? Why me? Will I ever have a baby? I'm constantly being reminded of what I lost, I can't help but feel jealous when I hear someone else is pregnant. It's immature, I know, but I'm tired of hearing how God works in mysterious ways and maybe it's for the better." Samantha looked up at Derek and met his gaze. There was something about this man that put her at ease. She felt comfortable with him, enough to open up and express herself more than she had with any other man besides John.

"Sam, I'm no expert, but I'm sure everything you felt and feel is normal. And with today's technology…"

"John doesn't believe in the whole in-vitro thing. He thinks it should just happen naturally. He entertained the idea just to make me happy, but I knew he wouldn't follow through."

"Well, you never know. Maybe he just doesn't understand completely. We are men after all." Derek smirked, trying to lighten the mood.

"Don't start sticking up for him, Derek. The bro code doesn't work in this situation. Besides, I thought you were on my side." Samantha managed a playful smile. "I used to go the park just to watch kids play. This one time, there was this little boy, he couldn't have been more than three years old, he was yelling for his mother to push him on the swing; she was too busy on her phone. She completely ignored him; finally the little boy gave up and went to the sand box. My heart broke for him. How could someone ignore their child like that?"

Derek shook his head and shrugged his shoulders.

"I just want what I had with my mom. We were so close, she did everything she could for us after my dad left. I was young, but I knew about his affairs. He was just never happy. My mother was devastated, but she never talked badly about him to me, she always put on a happy face. He didn't deserve her; she was too good for him." Samantha twirled her mother's bracelet around her wrist. She wiped the tears that streamed down her face. "I'm sorry; here I go again with all my problems. Wait, why did you come over? I know it wasn't to hear me cry again."

"I don't mind. Are you sure you're ok?"

Samantha nodded her head to reassure him. Derek stood from his chair and placed his mug in the sink. He turned around and leaned on the counter. "I uh, I came to actually apologize for ignoring you the past few days."

"So, you were ignoring me then?" Samantha teased, enjoying where this conversation was heading. By his body language she could tell he was uncomfortable and needed to tell her something. She was hoping it was what she had wanted to hear. As wrong as it was, she wanted him to admit his feelings about their attraction.

"Well, maybe a little. I know it was childish, but I really needed time away from you to clear my head. The thing is, I know what it's like to always come second. All through college, and our marriage, Lizzie was always so focused. I respect that and I'm proud of my wife, she worked hard for everything, but she doesn't know how to relax. I thought moving here would help us, rather than push us farther apart. Lizzie is putting in more time than expected at the hospital and I'm here, spending all my free time with you. Don't get me wrong, I have a good time with you, Sam, I just think I need to concentrate on getting everything in order at home, and with the baby coming…"

"Derek, I totally understand. You don't need to explain yourself. You don't think I have my doubts? I question everything. It's normal."

"I know, but the point is we're adults and we can't let this go any further. I like you, Sam, you're different, you make me feel alive, but…I just wanted to clear the air."

Samantha sat at the table processing everything Derek had just said. He was a man who knew how to express himself, a straight shooter. Sam respected him for that. It was one of the things that first attracted her to him. She knew not to press him anymore. The last thing she wanted to do was have him run in fear of her. Samantha realized she needed to be patient with him. This was a man with integrity, a man with morals. She would have to relax and let him come to her.

"No worries, the air is clear!" Samantha stood up and put away the milk and sugar. As she turned around, she noticed the look on Derek's face. His expression reminded her of a boy that had just lost his puppy. She couldn't decide if he really believed what he said or was just trying to convince himself.

CHAPTER FIFTEEN

It was a rare occasion that John was home early from work. They had eaten dinner and were about to get ready for bed when they heard a knock at the door. Samantha and John looked at one another, puzzled. Who could be knocking this late?

"Sorry to bother you, I just needed to ask a favor," Elizabeth stood in their front doorway looking a little disheveled and tired.

"No, not at all, what can we do for you? Is everything ok?"

"I hope so. Derek and I are leaving first thing in the morning to fly back to Florida. His dad is sick and we need to go as soon as we can. He fell down a flight of stairs and is in bad shape according to the doctor. He's in ICU and Derek is a wreck. I wanted to see if you can take in our mail and just keep your eye on the house for us while we're gone." Elizabeth was clearly distracted and was speaking so fast John was having a hard time keeping up with her. He nodded to let her know that it was alright. "Here's an extra key in case of an emergency. We should be back in a few days, or at least I'll be back, but…are you sure it's ok? I hate to be a bother. I am so sorry to come over this late. My God, with the baby and everything…"

"Not a problem, I'll let Samantha know and she'll take care of it for you. Everything will be ok. But Elizabeth, you need to calm down. We're here if you need anything. Don't worry about a thing." John reached out and gently touched her shoulder.

"Thank you so much, John. We'll know more once we get there."

"Ok, well no worries, we'll take in the mail and please, keep us posted."

"I will. Thank you so much. I don't know what we would have done if we didn't have you and Sam. I am so grateful to you both."

"Don't worry about a thing. Go home and take care of your family."

"Who was that?" Samantha asked when John returned to the den. She knew it had been Elizabeth, but couldn't hear the whole conversation. What on earth was going on? Surely Derek hadn't confessed to his wife. No, John looked too cool.

"Elizabeth. She left a house key in case of an emergency; they need to leave in the morning. Derek's father is in the hospital and they need to fly back to Florida right away."

"What? How long are they going for? What happened?" Samantha blurted out question after question. Feeling a little relieved and sad for Derek, she was also trying not to feel selfish that she wouldn't be able to see him.

"From what she said he fell and he's in the ICU. She was barely holding it together. Besides, I didn't want to ask too many questions. I was trying to calm the pregnant lady down. Jeez, what is with the third degree? Just take in the mail. I'm sure they'll keep us posted."

The next morning Samantha waited for John to leave for work before making her way across the street. What's the harm, right? They did give me a key. It's not like I'm breaking and entering, for Christ sake. I have a key, an open invitation to go on in. No harm in looking around. But maybe I should wait for the mailman to come first. That could be later this afternoon, she thought. I can't wait that long. She looked to see what neighbors were around in order to not cause any suspicion. The last thing she needed was Mrs. Kowalski asking what she was doing. Old bat is always in everyone's business. Thank God she was as old as the bible, otherwise people might believe her crazy stories. Samantha imagined her talking with the other neighbors. "You won't believe what I saw today. I would watch your husbands, ladies. If you only knew who was at whose house at the oddest time." Many times Samantha had wanted to tell her to shut up when she would gossip about other people, but she knew she couldn't. Samantha also knew that everyone on the block thought she was a conspiracy theorist fruitcake and didn't believe a word she said. If they only knew that the windbag was telling the truth.

As Samantha walked in, she spotted Elizabeth's workbag and Derek's sneakers on the floor. There was also a scent of disinfectant and Pledge in the air. What a "cozy little home" she muttered to herself. The house still needed some decorating. "Well, Elizabeth's never home, what man is going to take the initiative with picking out wall colors and throw rugs?" Samantha said out loud while touching the love seat that Derek had been sitting in the first time they met. She noticed that they still had a few boxes to unpack here and there. Stacked in the corner were boxes marked 'kitchen' and 'bedroom.' "Hmmm, now that's a room I haven't seen."

Samantha slowly walked towards the stairs. With each step she looked at every family photo hung neatly on the wall. Derek and Elizabeth's wedding photo, white fitted strapless dress, Swarovski crystal beading all the way down the front, her hair styled in an up-do, Derek in his black tux, shiny shoes, and the two facing each other holding hands with beaming smiles. Samantha couldn't help but feel a bit jealous of their relationship. They sure looked happy and in love. All smiles, all glowing. And now they were expecting their first baby. Why couldn't she have that too? She had a happy marriage but why were her babies taken from her? *Why can't I have it all? What does Elizabeth have that I don't?* Samantha stopped suddenly in her tracks; she had heard shuffling coming from the back of the house. Her pulse started to race and she could hear her heart pounding in her ears. *Shit, what was that? They can't be home. How would I explain being in here?* She slowly crept back down the stairs and tip-toed towards the kitchen; she peeked her head around the wall, her eyes roaming the room. Silence. Suddenly a loud bang and the cry of a cat rang through and made her jump. She crouched down and scurried over to peek out the kitchen back door window and saw Mrs. Kowalski's cat pounce off the metal trash bins chasing a squirrel. Her body relaxed and she laughed at herself for being so ridiculous. *Friggin' fur ball!* She turned on her heel and went back upstairs.

Derek's office was the first door right in front of her. It was the picture of him in cap and gown accepting his diploma that she couldn't keep her eyes off. She stood there in the doorway staring at it for a minute and then surveyed the rest of the room. It was a decent size, big enough for his bookshelf lined with leather bound novels of a few authors she recognized and a few she had never heard of. The desk was big and made of mahogany with carved edges. The computer sat in the middle with the printer on the left side. A Star Wars screen saver of Bobba Fett's Slave 1 ship was sliding across the screen; she smiled to herself remembering how he had gone on and on about how it was one of his favorite movies. *What a dork!* She noticed all his diplomas hung on the wall in a perfect line; this was just as she had pictured his office; grand and masculine. On the desk sat a picture of Elizabeth looking back at the camera smiling. *It must be nice to be you, Elizabeth. Who wouldn't want an adoring hot man at their side? Such an awesome life you have. And now you get to add the perfect baby boy to complete your picture perfect life.* Samantha could feel her eyes welling up. *Stop, Sam.* She walked over to the desk and ran her fingers across the back of the leather chair. She swung it around and delicately sat in it as if savoring the moment. Here he sits day after day working on his novel staring out this window. This is the window. *This must be what he sees when he looks out. My home. And me. He is staring* at me. *Watching me day after day. Wondering what excuse he can use to come over and chat. This is where it started. This is OUR secret.* She sat there a few minutes longer and a thought hit her. She knew she shouldn't, but she wanted, and needed to see.

Samantha continued down the hall to the door on the left. *Just open it, Sam. Just do it.* She took a deep breath and opened the door to the baby's nursery. It was painted the perfect pale baby blue with a yellow border. There stood an oak crib positioned against the far wall with the changing table across the room. They had started decorating with a baby sports theme. Of course. The crib bedding was blue and brown with a little teddy bear holding a baseball bat and ball in its other hand, the words 'slam,' 'home run' and 'strike' stitched into the edges. On the wall were decorative sports decals shaped as a mitt, and words saying 'All-Star.' Samantha walked across to the window where the wooden rocker was positioned in the corner. It had a navy blue cushion and cushioned fabric around the arms. A baby blanket was thrown over embroidered with the words 'Little Slugger.' Knowing that she shouldn't, Samantha sat down and rocked a bit, looking around the nursery. She closed her eyes, wondering what her baby girl's room would have looked like. She started to hum to herself. *What am I doing? Why do this to yourself Sam? Fresh Start. How am I to have a fresh start if I never face the truth? But not here, not now.* She tried to get up and walk out, but she couldn't. She was lost in the moment. *But this is not your moment Sam; this is some other woman's moment. Some other woman gets to have your perfect family.* And it wasn't fair. She was so close to having her dream to just have it taken.

Preterm labor. Samantha could hear the words over and over in her head haunting her. The doctors couldn't give her straight answers as to why. She was to accept it and move on. *Dammit! I don't want to accept it. I want my baby girl. But if I can't have my baby I can find something else to pass the time. Something else to take that isn't mine.*

Just then she felt a buzzing in her pant pocket, quickly forcing her back to reality. Samantha wiped the tears away from her face. She barely noticed she was crying and answered her cell. "Hi, hon, what's going on?" She tried to sound as if nothing was wrong.

"I was just calling to say not to wait up, looks like I'm going to be late again, sorry." John said. Samantha felt disappointed. She so desperately wanted to say, I need you. I need you to be home with me tonight, but she knew she couldn't ask. She already knew the answer. She just didn't want to feel as if she was about to lose to his job, again.

"Ok, I guess we're not going out to dinner then, huh?"

"No, I'm sorry, but I'll make it up to you another night. Hey, you ok? You sound… I don't know a little off. Something wrong?"

"No, I'm ok. Everything is fine. Alright, I'll see you when you get home. I'm sorry. I just have a little headache, that's all."

"Well then, I better get going." John hesitated. "Love ya."

"I love you too." Samantha hung up her phone. Time to go home she thought. She looked around at her surroundings, took a deep breath and walked out of the nursery, looking back only to make sure everything was as she found it. She didn't

121

realize that she had carefully placed a picture of Derek that had been sitting on the baby's dresser in the pocket of her jeans.

CHAPTER SIXTEEN

Sitting on her bed staring at the picture of Derek, Samantha was confused and bewildered. *How did I manage to take a picture from the Miller's home and put it in my pocket and not remember? What was I thinking? I wasn't. I must have seen it there and just taken it. Now what? How do I put it back in their home without being noticed?* The Millers were home. She heard the car pull up late the other night. She no longer had a reason to be in their home alone. *Sam, you're an idiot. Maybe with all the commotion they won't even notice. Who am I kidding? Elizabeth is going to notice a picture of her husband missing. Well, I can't do anything about it now. Deny. That's what I'll do if they ever question me. Deny.* Now that that's settled, Samantha took the picture of Derek and examined it further.

What a man, she thought. Here he was in his Florida baseball jersey looking so handsome, his muscular arms filling out the jersey in all the right places. *My God, he is so good-looking;*

his blue eyes were shining with pride as he accepted an award for something. Must be for his writing, she assumed. His smile was captivating. She thought back to the barbeque where they kissed in her kitchen. His kiss had been warm and inviting. She could have stayed in that place in time forever. It was the first time in a long time that she had felt desired. She was so deep in thought, she barely heard the knock on her front door.

"Sam? Sam? You in here?" It was Derek downstairs in her foyer calling for her. "I'm here! I'm upstairs, come on up!" she called out to him. Thank God I wore my old overall shorts. Lauren would not approve, but they were old and comfortable and had lots of pockets. And right at this moment she needed those pockets. She quickly shoved the picture of Derek into the side pocket. She heard his footsteps coming up the stairs. Sam quickly glanced into the mirror and fixed her hair. Derek reached her bedroom door and caught Sam looking in the mirror. "God, you're beautiful!" he whispered.

Samantha turned around and saw Derek standing in her bedroom doorway with two ventis from Starbucks.

"Hey, stranger!" Samantha smiled.

Derek cleared his throat. "I wanted to thank you for bringing in the mail and watching the house for us." He didn't move from the doorway.

"Oh, it was nothing. Come in, how's your dad? From the look on your face I take it he's ok?"

"He is. Thank you. He's on the mend."

"Oh, thank goodness, I know how close you are with him."

"I, um, brought you a Starbucks, your favorite. Caramel Mocha with no whip, fat free milk, and extra hot." He held it out to her with pride. Samantha felt warm inside. *Does John even know how I like my coffee?*

"Mmm, thank you. You didn't have to, but you know I will never pass up a Starbucks, especially when a good-looking man is paying." She giggled. She wasn't paying attention and for a moment forgot about the picture in her pocket until she saw it sliding out. It fell onto the ground right in front of Derek's feet. She gasped. *Shit, now what?* Samantha needed to think fast. She rushed over to Derek drawing his attention to her while managing to kick the picture under the dresser. As she reached for the coffee, their hands touched, sending sparks through her entire body. She knew he felt it too. Just as he went to say something she did the only thing she could think of and planted a kiss on the corner of his mouth. When Samantha took a step back, her cheeks began to redden. That one little kiss had sent shivers down her spine. She looked at Derek, all she saw was desire in his eyes.

He placed the coffees on the dresser and turned to face her. She knew what his next move would be, and she had no intention of stopping him. Derek slowly raised his hand to her cheek, stroking it gently. She looked up at him through her long lashes and smiled. He leaned in and kissed her. Samantha fell into his embrace and before she knew it they were grabbing at one another. This was what she wanted, but she needed to hear from him that he was ok with it. She stopped kissing him and pushed away.

"I can't, w-we can't. We both agreed never again."

Derek took a step closer, trying to bridge the gap between them. "I know what we said, but I can't stop thinking about you, the kiss we shared, that night in my truck. I just realized how much I missed you these past few days while I was away from you. I can't stop feeling this way and I know you feel it too."

"What way, Derek? We're friends, neighbors. What changed your mind? You were right, we need to act like adults; maybe you should just go. This is not good, we're playing with fire." Samantha stood at the foot of the bed, resting her hands on her hips. She didn't really want Derek to leave, but she had to be sure this was really something he could go through with. And she needed him to play by her rules. Otherwise she needed to end this once and for all before it went any further. The last thing she needed was to make another mistake that needed to be covered up.

"Leave? You want me to leave? Really? Because you were right there with me, kissing me back. And I know you enjoyed it." He was grinning. That damn dimple. "If you want me to go I will. We can just pretend like this never happened, but I can't keep lying to myself anymore. Tell me, is that what you want?"

Samantha turned away. "You're right, I did enjoy the kiss." She crossed her arms across her chest, knowing all the right moves to entice him into playing her game. She had the innocent act down to a science. "This could end badly for us. What if they find out?"

Derek closed the distance between them, resting his hands on her shoulders. Samantha looked back at him with the most seductive look in her eyes, letting him know that it was alright to proceed. He turned her around to face him; taking both her hands, he guided her towards the bed. Gently he pushed her down, holding both of her hands, lifting them above her head. He crouched down and kissed her. He started off slow and soft, but as their lips parted and their tongues met, the kisses grew hard and passionate. Samantha felt her body respond to him immediately; she felt a heated ache between her legs as his kisses trailed down her chin to her neck. He found the sensitive spot just below her ear and a low moan escaped her throat. "Oh, God."

His hands trailed along the side of her body; he cupped her breast over her shirt and squeezed gently. Slowly, his hand moved underneath her back to unclip her bra. He undid the clips of her overalls and chuckled. "Hey, they're comfortable."

He just looked at her with a grin and continued to lift her shirt up. He began kissing her breasts; her nipples tightened at the touch of his tongue. There was something about the way Derek touched her, the soft wet feel of his tongue on her bare skin, it ignited a flame inside and sent shivers throughout her entire body. Samantha sat up slightly so he could finish removing her tank top; he tossed it on the floor along with his own. Derek trailed his kisses from one breast to the other. Samantha ran her fingers through the little curls on top of his head. Being with him was better than she could have imagined. He knew just where to touch her and how. This was finally happening, Samantha was lost in pure bliss as she lay there with Derek.

"Mmm, Sam" Derek whispered as he tugged on her nipple with his teeth.

Samantha let out another moan, reaching to pull Derek up to kiss her. "Oh god, you're so hot," he moaned into her mouth.

"How bad do you want it?" Samantha whispered as she kissed his neck and nibbled on his ear.

In one swift movement Derek grabbed the rest of Samantha's denim overalls at the waist and pulled them down. Samantha began to snicker "That bad, huh?"

Derek looked at her, raising his eyebrows and smiled, showing off his sweet dimple.

"Your turn, Mr. Miller," Samantha smirked. He stood up and unbuttoned his jean shorts; Samantha's eyes followed Derek's movement, watching his erection spring out of his boxer shorts. She giggled as he tossed them on the floor. "Mmm, Derek, you just keep getting better and better." Samantha kneeled up waiting for him to join her back on the bed; he sat down on the edge of the mattress allowing Samantha to straddle him wearing nothing but her white silk thong; her hand traveled down from his chest to his stomach, tracing the thicker curls to the thin hairline on his flat hard stomach. Derek smiled.

She took all of him into her hand and began stroking. Derek let out a low growl and Samantha grinned down at him. "You like that?" she whispered flirtatiously.

"Mmm, very much so." Samantha leaned down and took him into her mouth. Her lips covered his erection while her hand continued to stroke him. After a few minutes of pleasure Derek pulled Samantha down to lie next to him. They rolled on their sides facing each other, kissing. Derek had one arm under Samantha's back while the other reached between her thighs and under her thong. She was hot and ready for him; her body ached with desire. She leaned into his touch, but Derek wanted to take his time and caress every inch of her.

"Derek, I want you now, please don't make me beg," Samantha whispered, breathless.

"Oh baby, I'm just getting started."

"Started? You better hurry up before I reach the finish line without you!"

Derek laughed. "I guess in that case, do you have any condoms?"

Samantha stopped for a moment to think. "Hold on" she said as she stepped off the bed and ran into the master bath. Derek could hear her opening and closing drawers and pushing aside the contents searching for what she needed. Within a few minutes, she returned grinning, holding a little foiled square wrapper.

Samantha snuggled up to him as he laid down next to her and rolled on the condom. Derek sat up and pulled off her panties, their eyes locked as he positioned his hips to fit tightly between her thighs and pushed himself inside her. Samantha wrapped her legs around his waist and they began to move and rock into one another. She grabbed Derek's hips, pulling him deeper inside of her, she cried out Derek's name while he arched his back, groaning, pushing as deep as he could.

129

"Sam, I can't tell you how long I've fantasized about this, what it felt like to touch you, be inside you." He leaned down and began to kiss her intensely.

Samantha couldn't get any closer to Derek than she was now, but it wasn't enough; him being inside her only made her crave more of him. Her orgasm was building fast, quicker than it ever had. She was extremely turned on, and knew he was too. She could feel him fighting the urge to climax. Once her legs began to quiver underneath him and she dug her nails into his back, Derek thrust inside her one last time. She loved how his entire body spasmed as he called out her name.

Afterwards they were both entwined together. He reached over and touched her cheek. She grabbed his hand and kissed it. They knew what this meant. They were now having an affair. For the first time, Samantha thought she felt guilt surfacing, but pleasure had taken over and she was not turning back. From the expression on Derek's face, she thought he might have a harder time.

"I better get going. I don't want to leave, but I need to get the next chapter of my book sent to the editor. I wasn't expecting to stay this long when I came with the coffee." Derek grinned and started to get up. Sam sat up watching him, she was fascinated by him. Every fantasy she had about Derek was nothing compared to what she had just experienced.

"It's ok, I totally understand. I have so many errands to run."

Sam watched as Derek discarded the condom. Luckily, she and John hadn't gone through the box they had bought after the miscarriages; they'd needed to take precautions for a few months before trying again.

Derek pulled his shirt over his head; he walked around to the other side of the bed and bent down to kiss her. When they stopped she looked at him with a girly grin, "Mr. Miller, I must say that was pretty amazing. Remember, no strings attached. I wouldn't want you to fall in love with me. That's a no-no."

He smiled back at her. "Not bad for a pencil pusher, huh? And Mrs. Bennett, you should worry about yourself, now that you've sampled the goods I'm a hard a man to forget but I agree, no strings attached." He scooped up his pants from the floor and put them on. "Mrs. Bennett, you are pretty amazing." With that he bent down to grab his sneakers. From the corner of his eye he noticed the item that had flown out of Samantha's pocket earlier. He took a quick glance and noticed what looked like the colors of his Florida Rays jersey. Odd, he thought. He then turned back around to Samantha who was standing in front of him, naked and smiling. He forgot all about the piece of paper under the dresser.

"See you later?" she asked. All Derek could do was wink, grab his coffee off the dresser and walk out of the room.

After she heard the front door shut, Samantha quickly ran to the dresser. She scooped up the picture and flattened it out. *That was close, Sam. Quick thinking, getting his attention by standing there naked. What man wouldn't take note? But still, what if he saw it? If he had, he would have said something. It was all crumpled up anyway, he wouldn't know what it was.* Sure of this, Samantha walked into her closet and reached up to the top shelf and pulled down her locked box. She then went over to the back of the closet and found the shoe box that held her wedding shoes. She opened the box and took her Louis Vuitton shoes out and gently pulled out the tissue paper to find the key. She used the key to open the locked box and placed the picture of Derek in it. Here he was safe with all her other possessions.

CHAPTER SEVENTEEN

"Dinner was delicious, babe," John said, putting his plate in the double sink. He looked over at Samantha who was cleaning up from dinner singing to herself.

"*Yeah baby you're the right kind of wrong, Might be a mistake—* What?" Samantha glanced over at John who was watching in amusement.

"Nothing, just waiting for you to tell me what's up with you." He smiled.

"Nothing's up. Why do you say that?"

"You just…you seem different lately, happier, you're singing!" John laughed.

Samantha continued to clean off the table and walk around John, placing more dishes and silverware in the sink. "Well, don't you want me to be happier, a fresh start?" She said while making quotation marks with her fingers.

"Oh, hun, of course, I love seeing you like this." John reached for Samantha's hands. "Does this mean you want to start trying again?" Pulling his wife into a hug he began to snuggle inside the crook of her neck. "I haven't really thought about it," Samantha answered lightly.

"Maybe we can start trying again…like tonight," John said, looking at her, wiggling his eyebrows up and down in the playful way he always did with Samantha to make her laugh. She had the most infectious laugh and her smile was the thing John always said he loved most; he told her it was what made him fall in love with her so many years ago.

"I'm beginning to feel like myself again. It feels good," she said, curling into John's arms and resting her head on his chest. Closing her eyes, she could still feel Derek's touch. *I shouldn't be thinking about another man's touch while I'm in my husband's arms.*

"You know I don't mind waiting a little longer to try again. I'm alright with whatever choice you make." John never pushed the issue, but she didn't know what she wanted at the moment. At this moment she was enjoying her time with Derek and she wasn't too sure about anything but the present. She just looked at her husband, and thought she should feel guilty but she didn't. She almost felt justified with her choices. For so long she had played second fiddle to John's career. He worked long hours and went on last-minute business trips. Sometimes she couldn't even say goodbye. She knew he loved her, but she also knew that his work was her competition. His work was his mistress. *How's that for irony?*

"John, we don't have to make any decisions now, do we? I think we should just enjoy life and spend time with our friends. Have some fun! Whatever happens, happens. Let's just throw caution to the wind and relax." She twirled around, laughing.

"Speaking of fun and enjoying our friends, I think you're enjoying the new company during the day." Samantha froze, *he couldn't possibly know!*

"The Millers, you know, hanging out with them, coffee with Derek, shopping with Lizzie, I think it's great. Let's hope they stay."

Samantha pulled away and walked back over to the dinner table. "We can only hope. But enough about them, that's ancient history. But, yeah, it is nice. Not as lonely anymore, you know? It's great to make new friends." She gave him a half-smile. "And by the way, I'll have to take a rain check on that offer of yours. I have an early morning aerobics class. You know I have to keep my girly figure."

"Aha, so I take it I'm not getting lucky tonight? Alright, you get a pass tonight, but next time you're mine, baby. Oh, by the way I have an overnight trip for work coming up. I should find out the details this week. And tomorrow night I'll be late again, I'm sorry." He swatted her ass as he headed into the den to relax a bit before bed. Samantha watched him.

There is my husband, hardworking, dedicated and loving. Of course she knew how to pull his strings and keep a handle on him. But all these late nights and trips took their toll on a marriage. Scheduling intimacy with your husband just wasn't romantic. She loved him, and appreciated everything he did to provide for them, she just needed and desired more.

Once the kitchen was cleaned, Samantha headed upstairs to change into her pajamas and check her mail that she'd been neglecting over the past few days. She sat in John's office at his dark cherry wood desk in the large black leather chair. He very rarely worked from home but they had the spare room and decided it was worth having it for when the baby came. John would be able to try and spend more time at home to help her as they didn't have much family around to help. John's folks were older now and lived out of state and Lauren was all Samantha had. Now it was just an empty office.

Guess I'm not as popular as I thought. She quickly scrolled down the list and saw her usual emails from Lauren and a few bits of spam. But there was another email that immediately perked her up when she saw who it was from.

Subject:

Time: 5:34pm

From: Derek Miller <MrWrite5 @gmail.com>

To: Samantha Bennett<Greeneyez@gmail.com>

Hey! Was thinking about you. Have a great night.

Samantha smiled as the butterflies flew around inside her stomach. She hit reply and a new message box opened:

Subject:

Time: 9:18pm

From: Samantha Bennett<Greeneyez@gmail.com>

To: Derek Miller <MrWrite5 @gmail.com>

Same to you Mr. Miller. ;)

She thought about writing more but decided to leave him hanging on. It was always best that way. She chuckled to herself with satisfaction. She then emailed Lauren back, closed the computer down and went to bed. *I wonder what's in store for me tomorrow. Well whatever it is I'm going to enjoy it. My fresh start is waiting.*

CHAPTER EIGHTEEN

Derek and Samantha lay tangled up in the sheets of his dark wood sleigh bed. Today was a little different than most days. Derek was the one to offer Samantha coffee, and they had ended up in his bed rather than hers.

"This is pretty. I like the way the chain is roped and connects to the stones," he said as he swirled the bracelet on Samantha's wrist.

"Thank you, it was my mother's. She never took it off. It was the last gift my father gave her before he left us. I never take it off; it helps me remember the good times we shared before he ran off." Samantha leaned up on her elbows and tilted her head, looking over at Derek. He brushed a long strand of hair away from her face and tucked it behind her ear. "She gave it to me before she passed; it was a few months before my high school graduation. She was my best friend; it was always just me and her, until we moved in with my aunt and uncle. If it wasn't for them, I don't know where I'd be today. It's really the only piece I have left of her." Samantha's voice softened and her eyes shifted to the bracelet.

Derek listened to every word she spoke. He could see the hurt in her eyes and wanted to comfort her, but he didn't want to press. "Well, I'm sure she was a beautiful women, she raised you, didn't she?"

"That's sweet, thank you. I am pretty awesome, if I say so myself." Derek grabbed her, pulling her in for a kiss. She pulled back and smirked. "I'm ready to go again, how 'bout you, Mr. Miller?" Samantha sat up and traced her fingers down the side of his stomach.

"Oh, you have no idea how ready I am." Derek shifted on the mattress, about to kiss her again when she stood up. Derek couldn't help but drool over this perfect naked women standing in front of him, a woman that he had just made love to and who he was about to have again. He just couldn't get enough of her.

"First you have to catch me." Samantha winked and laughed as she darted for the bedroom door. Derek jumped off the bed and chased after her down the hall.

He followed behind her down the stairs, through the living room, where they stopped, standing across from one another with nothing but an arm chair between them, daring the other to make the first move.

"Hey, what's that?"

"Oh, I'm not falling for that one!"

Trying her hardest to be sexy and put a little distance between them, she ran towards the stairs, Samantha's foot caught on the last step and she tripped on the landing, her knee catching the fall. Derek was right behind her, but before he could ask if she was alright, Samantha was gasping for air from laughing so hard that she couldn't control a snort from escaping. Derek shook his head and laughed along with her. "Let me help you up, Miss Piggy."

Samantha opened her mouth to say something but nothing came out; all she could do was pout.

"Really, it's cute."

He grabbed her hand and helped her up, pinning her against the hallway wall. While both of them were trying to catch their breath, he kissed her. His kisses were soft and sensual before their lips parted and his tongue collided with hers. The kiss grew hungrier and Samantha grabbed the back of his neck and pulled him in closer. Derek's hands traced the side of her body and around to grab her ass, his erection was hard between them. His pulse raced and he guided her through the hallway back towards the bedroom still locked at the lips.

Just as they reached the bed, Samantha heard keys jingling in the front door. Her stomach flipped, she stood there frozen. She nudged him off her. "Derek, is someone here?"

Derek glanced behind him at the clock, not really worried because he knew his wife was at work and he wasn't expecting anyone. He turned back to kiss Samantha, but she was already standing on the other side of the bed, in her sundress, trying to make the bed as neat as possible. That was when he heard the front door swing open and Elizabeth call out.

His stomach dropped and he darted for his shorts and t-shirt. His heart started to pound, and he couldn't think clearly. His body was on auto pilot, he was dressed within seconds and Samantha did her best with the sheets. Derek ran to his doorway; he heard Elizabeth in the kitchen opening and closing cabinets. He waved his hand for Samantha to come with him. They tiptoed down the hall into the baby's nursery. Samantha had to cover her mouth to prevent herself from giggling out loud. She knew it wasn't funny, but nerves got the best of her. Derek put a finger up to his lips and looked at her with wide eyes, pleading with her to stop laughing. Once Samantha was inside the nursery he stood in the hallway and called out to his wife. "Hey, Lizzie, I'm just showing Sam the baby's room, why you home so early?"

Elizabeth waddled over to the bottom of the stairs. "I told you I had a half day today, did you forget?" She rolled her eyes and headed back into the kitchen while calling out a quick hello to their neighbor. Derek let out a sigh of relief, how could he have forgotten? He glanced at Samantha, smiled and went downstairs to greet his wife.

Left alone Samantha's eyes roamed the room; her church giggles stopped immediately, her heart started to pound but for different reasons now; it felt like yesterday that she had rocked in this chair dreaming about her little girl in another woman's home. *What the hell was she doing? That was close. Too close and now look where I ended up, not in Derek's sheets again, but in the baby's nursery!*

CHAPTER NINETEEN

"Hey, girl." Lauren was waving her hand at her best friend as she walked in the restaurant and headed over to their usual table. "Hey." Samantha stood up to hug Lauren.

The young bus boy set down a glass of water in front of Lauren as she hung her purse on the chair and sat across from Samantha.

"Oh, can I get an ice tea, please?" Lauren smiled at the young man as he turned to leave.

"Sorry, I was held up with a customer. Were you waiting long?" Lauren sighed as she took a long sip of her water.

"I actually just got here a few minutes ago and placed our order. I knew you wouldn't have enough time; and would probably have to head back to the bank so…"

"Mmm, I'm starving!" Lauren lifted her water to take another sip. "We cannot go this long without our lunch dates" She looked up and gave a frown. The bus boy brought Lauren's Ice tea and another for Samantha. "I don't remember why we even stopped going to Zorba's, but I'm glad you found this place, it's so delish!"

Samantha remembered that day so clearly; she needed a good reason as to why they couldn't continue their lunch dates at Zorba's anymore. Luckily, when she found this place she was able to convince Lauren to try it without ever explaining why she didn't want to return to Zorba's.

Trying to change the subject she said, "So what happened at the doctor's the other day?"

"Uh, I was due for my annual, but my normal doctor had some kind of emergency so after having to wait for what felt like forever, they finally squeezed me in with another doctor after complaining so much." Lauren lifted her glass to take another sip. "Mmm, you have no idea, I'm sitting on the table waiting again, and I feel like I need to pee even though I just went, I hate that, probably nerves, so anyway, I was about to use the bathroom when I heard the knock on the door and in walked Dr. Matthews."

Samantha sat smiling, listening to her friend go on and on about her visit. She couldn't help it, Lauren had a way of telling a story that drew you in. "All I wanted was for the floor to open up and suck me in right then and there. You know me, Sam, I don't embarrass easy…total babe and he couldn't have been much older than us. I swear, I was mortified!"

Samantha began to chuckle. She and Christie would tease Lauren about her flaring arms, they swore one day someone would be knocked out by them during a story telling.

"I wasn't prepared either, if I had known I would have done a better job trimming and brought lotion or spray…something. God…my usual doctor is an older man; I don't need to put the effort in when I see him. Then to top it off, I had to shift closer to the edge, almost falling off the table, and when he went to swab me, the metal clamp grazed my lower inner thigh and I jumped. *Really*, who does that? The nurse and the doctor both could barely hide their smiles. I just wanted to die."

At this point Lauren and Samantha were laughing loud enough that other customers began to turn and stare in curiosity, especially when Samantha let out a snort. She had to wipe away the tears that fell down her face from laughing so hard.

The waiter brought over the large Greek salad, along with the platter of fries, pita bread and extra yogurt sauce. He placed two plates down in front of each of them. "Can I get you anything else, ladies?"

"No, thank you" Samantha answered. "Lau, you're so animated when telling a story, I've missed you." Both girls laughed some more and dug into their meal. Lauren continued with her story while Samantha started to drift back to the other day with Derek. This little affair was becoming a daily routine; she hadn't expected it to move so fast. She nodded at her best friend at all the right places but she was fidgety. She so wanted to tell her what was going on. Just as Lauren was about to talk about her last date, Samantha's text message alert went off. She pulled out her chirping phone and couldn't help but feel all giddy inside when she saw it was from Derek.

Hey, I could really go for some coffee a little later, you game?

Samantha chuckled to herself and hit reply while grinning ear to ear.

So is that what we're calling it these days?

Derek immediately responded.

LOL ;)

Samantha replied again then returned her phone to her purse.

Ill text you when I get in a little later

Lauren tilted her head to the side and studied Samantha's face. "Sam, spill the beans, I know something's up with you. Here I am going on and on about my annual spread your legs exam and I haven't even asked what's going on with you? Something has you all flustered....OH MY GOD, are you pregnant?"

"What?" Samantha looked up "No Lau, it's only been a few months and John and I haven't really started to try again."

"Oh, honey, I'm sorry. I didn't mean...I just, here I go with my big ole mouth again...something's up with you lately though." Placing both elbows on the table in front of her and resting her face in both hands, Lauren let out a big sigh. "Was that John? Let me guess, he has something wonderful planned for you or he bought you a new piece of bling? My God, in my next life I want to come back as you, Sam!"

"Oh Lau, stop! It's not always sunshine, lollipops and rainbows, you know! Marriage isn't all it's cracked up to be. John is gone a lot. It gets lonely…" *Ding Ding* Samantha lost her train of thought as her cell went off again. "And you could stop being a bitch and give Vinny another chance. John said he's grown up and is looking to settle down."

She pulled out her phone and saw there was another message from Derek.

It's later, ;) Your coffee is getting cold….

Lauren rolled her eyes at Samantha over her glass of ice tea. "I'm so done with Vincent Vano; I don't know why you defend him so much. I'm done talking about that jerk." Samantha was trying to pay attention to the conversation but she wanted to message Derek back. She placed her phone on her lap and discretely typed back,

Patience young skywalker….I am sure you can find ways to heat me, I mean my coffee, up soon…

There that should keep him happy, Samantha thought as she listened to Lauren go on about what an ass Vin was. Then she startled Samantha with her next question. "How are the new neighbors? Well, mostly how is hot Derek?" Lauren fanned herself with her napkin. "Come on, you got to admit he is something to look at! If he wasn't married…What I would do to him…MmmmMmmmMmmm. And isn't Elizabeth due soon?"

Ding Ding Samantha just laughed at Lauren and brushed off her comments even though the very thought of him made her legs quiver. If she only knew that he was the one blowing up her phone waiting for their next encounter. "Um, I think so, I think actually within a few weeks, I'm surprised she hasn't gone into early labor with the amount of hours she puts in at the hospital." *Ding Ding Oh my God, now what?*

Young sky walker, huh? Does this mean you will be Princess Leia and I get a private showing of you in a gold bikini? (Minus the whole brother/sister connection! LOL) Mmmm…Now my coffee is heating up again! You better get here soon!

"Lau, they are great neighbors and becoming fast friends." *If she only knew how fast…* "But anyway, I am sorry it took so long to get together." Samantha read the message and laughed to herself.

"Oh no worries, besides Rich has me working a lot thanks to the new mortgage laws. Banking, it sucks! Did I tell you what happened?"

Samantha just nodded and Lauren went off about a customer that was a total bitch or something. She hit reply and quickly wrote:

Ha-ha, down boy! Believe me I want coffee just as bad as you. ;)

"So, what do you say about going out one weekend? I could totally use a night out dancing, who knows, maybe I'll get lucky!" Lauren put away her lipstick and swatted her newly painted lips. Looking down at her phone she panicked. "Shit, I need to get going, I'm already going to be late and Rich will have my ass. I need to cut back on my lunch hours to make up for the frigging doctors visit."

Samantha realized she had missed Lauren's bitch customer story and something about a night out, but in true Lauren fashion she didn't seem to notice. "Go... go, I'll take care of this, call me later on."

Grabbing her things, Lauren leaned down to give Samantha's shoulder a squeeze. "Mwah, thanks. I'll call you later!"

Ding Ding Samantha didn't need to look to see who it was from. It was all she needed to read to get her moving.

I'm waiting for you....Hurry baby....

Samantha threw money down on the bill and grabbed her things and left the restaurant. She knew exactly where she was going. This time she didn't respond; she didn't need to.

CHAPTER TWENTY

"John Bennett."

"Hey, babe, how's it going?" Samantha asked.

"Hi, Hun, work's busy, everything ok?" Samantha could tell by the tone of his voice that he was distracted. Better keep this quick, she thought.

"I'm good, I just wanted to call and say hello. Um, did you see Elizabeth or Derek this morning at all?"

"Ah, no…Why? Was I supposed to?"

"Well, I don't think Elizabeth went to work, both their cars have been home all morning."

"And? I don't get it." Samantha could already sense that she was pestering her husband and he was losing interest in this phone call. "Sam, are you joining in on the neighborhood watch? Please, we already have one Mrs. Kowalski; we don't need another meddler on the block. Besides, what they do is none of our business. Listen, babe, I have another call." Samantha could hear papers being shuffled and the tapping of a keyboard. *Typical, every time I call these days while he's at work he rushes me off for another call. Who is more important than his wife?* Samantha made a mental note to ask him next time they were alone.

"I'm just curious that's all. She works just as much as you, so it's not normal for her to be home on a Tuesday afternoon. Alright, you sound busy, so I'll let you go." Samantha sighed.

"Sorry, I'll call you later then, love you." John hung up without waiting for a reply.

Samantha looked out the front window for a bit staring across the street. *What is going on? If she went into labor, we would have known.* After the last few "coffee" dates Samantha was looking forward to this morning's 'coffee.' She had even picked out a great sexy outfit to wear (not that she was planning on wearing it for long). She was disappointed and mad at Elizabeth. "Gee, if you're not going to have that baby, then go to work! Screw him. It's a beautiful day, and I am not about to waste this outfit. I think I'll read on the front porch." She looked in the mirror. "Mmmm…too bad, Mr. Miller, look at what you're missing out on!" She blew a kiss, turned and grabbed her book and coffee and headed for the porch.

"Derek, can we chat for a minute?" Elizabeth leaned on the doorway of Derek's office.

"What's that?" Derek looked away from the window back at his wife. "I'm sorry, I was just, uh, clearing my head for a minute." Derek was watching Samantha sitting alone in her short denim mini skirt, white tank top, and no bra. She had her legs propped up on another chair. *Those legs, just yesterday they were wrapped around my waist while I had her propped up against the front door in the foyer. We didn't even make into the bedroom. What I wouldn't give to be across the street tangled up in the sheets with Sam at this moment!*

"HELLO! Earth to Derek…You alright?" she gave him a puzzled look. Derek turned from the window again and smiled at her. "You've been a bit distracted these days, something up?" He was still sitting there with a shit-eating grin, like a boy caught with his hand in the cookie jar. She was getting frustrated with him. "What are you looking at?" Elizabeth waddled over to the side of Derek's desk and looked out the window. She noticed Samantha sitting on her front porch, reading. "What is she wearing? If she spread her legs anymore the whole neighborhood would know what size undies she was wearing; if she is even wearing any! And my Lord, put a bra on!"

Elizabeth turned to face her husband. "Oh, now I get it. Nice view." She shot her husband a dirty look. "Must be nice to have all that free time. I don't understand why she just doesn't go back to work? I mean, didn't she miscarry a few months ago?" The only reaction she received was a blank stare. "Don't get me wrong, I like her and it is awful what happened, but I don't know…I can't believe John is ok with her just sitting around all day. And like THAT!"

Derek sat in his computer chair staring at his wife. He couldn't help feel annoyed and a little protective of Samantha.

153

What does she care what Sam does all day. "Lizzie, I don't think you're being fair. She had two miscarriages; she had to deliver one of them. Could you imagine? Delivering a baby girl, only to have her taken from you? I couldn't. I think she is a pretty strong woman for dealing with all that. And then to have a husband who is always at work, never there when she needs him. It must be rough." The compassion in his eyes for Samantha was more than Elizabeth could handle right then.

Elizabeth shot him a look of confusion. "Are you really defending her?" She could feel her blood begin to boil. "Hold on! Did you just use the words fair and rough for a women sitting on her ass reading a book without a care in the world? Really!" Elizabeth couldn't believe her ears. "I don't mean to be insensitive, Derek. Yes, it is tragic to have to go through that, but fair, FAIR? You want to talk about fair?" He looked at her in shock. " I'm nine months pregnant, swollen feet, about to pop, but I work long and hard hours all day, while you sit home doing *what* exactly?" She placed her hands on her hips waiting for a reply. Nothing. "Oh and ROUGH? Really? She has it rough! Sure, Derek, she looks so miserable sitting over there on her perch! Sitting there like a queen with barely any clothes on! Yeah, that's the rough life! The rest of us are working our asses off and she has it rough!" Her hands were balled into fists now as she watched Derek sit there with a blank stare. "What is wrong with you, am I missing something here?" She stood there waiting for a reaction, an apology, something that resembled remorse.

"Lizzie, you need to calm down, I think you're overacting, where is this anger coming from? What does Sam have to do with anything? I thought you two were friends? This isn't like you. You can't possibly be jealous of Sam? " He stood up and walked around the desk to comfort his wife. He knew he needed to calm the situation down and quick. He felt for his wife but he also wanted to be wrapped up in Samantha's arms, touching her. Actually he wanted to be anywhere but here at this moment discussing his lover with his pregnant wife. He knew he should feel guilty and a part of him did, but another part of him wanted Samantha more. So much more then he should. "Lizzie, please..." Elizabeth pushed his arm away and stormed out of his office and into the nursery. Derek followed close behind, groaning to himself. *Keep your cool, Derek, don't give her a reason to be suspicious, just calm her down.*

"What is the matter?" *Shit, have this baby soon, because these mood swings are killing me. No wonder I would rather be fucking the neighbor!*

She stopped short and whipped around to face him. Derek saw a look in her eyes that he had never seen before. Venom was pouring out of her pores. He knew he needed to extinguish this, but he also knew that she needed to let it out. She finally turned to him and spoke, her voice calm. "Let's re-cap, shall we? While I am at work busting my fat pregnant ass, you are here writing your 'book.' I know we agreed that I could handle the financial end of things, but lately I don't understand what is going on while I'm not here."

"What do you mean, when you're not here? Lizzie, I AM writing my book."

"Really, Derek? Then answer me this, why can't you do a simple list of things that I ask?" Tears began to fill her eyes. "We have boxes still left to be unpacked. Do you think they're going to unpack themselves? Oh wait, I know, your pregnant wife, after working twelve hour shifts, is supposed to unpack them?" Derek stood there with his mouth open, about to say something, but she didn't care at this point. She kept going, "This shelf I asked you to hang is still on the floor. Newsflash Derek, the baby is going to be here any day! What are you waiting for?" She held up a white decorative shelf, shaking it in front of Derek. "WHEN do you plan on hanging it, when the baby starts grade school? I need that shelf in order to finish the room, which obviously you don't care about since it's still sitting here! Oh, but you're too busy writing your book! Let's not interrupt the man from writing his precious fucking book!" She went to the dresser. "I have some books, the photos of us…" Elizabeth put down the shelf and began to open drawers on the changing table. "Where *is* that picture? I know it was here." Confusion set in. "I swear I left it in here on the dresser." She wiped away the few tears that streamed down her cheek. "I love that picture of you. Where the hell is it?" She was looking everywhere, behind the dresser, under the crib. She stopped to take a deep breath. She was looking out the window. There she saw what she had seen before, Samantha sitting there. She couldn't stop watching her. Something was eating at her and she started to panic.

156

Derek walked up behind her and started to rub her shoulder but she shrugged it away. "I'm sorry, honey. Really, I am." He looked over at the dresser, trying to recall where he had last seen the picture. Something was nagging at him. He had recently seen it, but couldn't remember where. "Honey, it's only a picture. We can get another one made up. It's no big deal. We have plenty of pictures of me in my baseball jersey." He let his words trail off as he thought for a minute; that was it, the baseball jersey, that particular color of blue. He had seen it and he remembered exactly where.

Elizabeth slowly turned around. "Derek, is something going on with you and Sam? Oh my God, are you having an affair?" She wiped away the last of her tears; she was holding her breath, fearing the answer. Her big brown eyes glared at him waiting for his response, praying it wasn't true. All of the anger had been building up inside. Now that she had said the words out loud, it made sense. It was as if the pieces of a puzzle were fitting perfectly. His distractions, the lack of work around the house, the constant coffee breaks, how could she have been so blind? She was about to have this man's baby, how could this be happening? Please, let me be wrong. She took a deep breath and looked at her husband.

"Derek, answer the question." She knew her husband inside and out and this time she couldn't get a read on his expression. She wasn't sure if she saw guilt or anger in his eyes.

"W-What Lizzie NO! What makes you - why would you even say that? You can't be serious!" He panicked a bit, caught off guard. "So because I was looking out a fucking window and

157

didn't hang a fucking shelf, I am now screwing the neighbor? Yes, that's it, Lizzie, when you aren't home, I am banging everyone on the block! Yep, you should see how Mrs. Kowalski likes it! Oh boy, she likes it rough, the old bat! I can bend the old bitch over on her walker and give it to her until she screams! That's me! I am the neighborhood stud! Fucking everything I can! You are SO smart Lizzie. You got it all figured out!" He laughed out loud. She stood there staring back at him.

"What am I supposed to think, Derek? You haven't touched me in weeks. I know I'm not as tempting lately with this huge belly but Derek, not even a kiss? Nothing? I can't blame you for looking at another woman when I look like this. But I can't help thinking that there is more going on here. When you're not writing, you're always over there drinking coffee. How much coffee do you need? What else are you two doing?" She looked at him, waiting for him to respond. He said nothing. "Derek, nothing is getting done around here. Can you blame me for thinking that something is going on? What happened to the man I married? Where is he? You're not the same man. You've changed and I'm not too sure if I like this new person." She sat down in the rocker and looked at Derek, waiting for him to answer her. When he still said nothing, she threw in one last dig. "Maybe Sam likes this new Derek but I sure as shit DON'T."

Derek started pacing the nursery floor, trying to remain calm. He took a deep breath and started to plead his case. "Lizzie, you can't be serious. We moved here for YOU, I had to put MY career on hold. Where is all this paranoia coming from?"

Elizabeth sat there with her arms folded, rocking and glaring at him. Derek was beginning to lose his temper. "Since you are now the head of the coffee committee, I would like to know, what is the big deal about having coffee with the neighbor? I didn't know it was a crime to have coffee, fucking arrest me!" He tried to calm himself, but she was looking at him like he was a piece of shit and it was infuriating. "So let me get this straight. Just so I know exactly what I am being accused of; I didn't hang your goddamn shelf, a picture is missing that I guess is my fault, I haven't finished unpacking the boxes, oh and the most offensive of all crimes, I had coffee with the neighbor! All of these are punishable crimes according to you! You are now the judge and jury! Hang me!"

Elizabeth started to say something but he hushed her and went on. "Oh no you don't! You don't get to sit here and unload on me and call me a cheat and not hear what I have to say. I just listened to you bitch about how I'm a changed man and how you don't like this new man. Let me tell you sweetheart, you ain't no fucking walk in the park lately either! Touch you! I don't touch you? You don't even allow me near you, ice princess! When was the last time you kissed me?"

She gave a blank stare.

"That's what I thought! You haven't! Don't pin our lack of intimacy all on me! All of this because I didn't hang a fucking shelf! Give me a fucking break! You think the baby is going to know the difference?" He boiled, his hands were balled in fists, he wrinkled his brow, his face turning bright red, he had never been more mad in his entire life. "I am sorry, Elizabeth, but I think you are looking to blame anyone for your attitude! And to blame Sam? What did she do but be a friend to you? Nice one, darling. Maybe you're the one that has changed! The old Lizzie wouldn't blame some innocent woman for her behavior! So don't turn this around on Sam and me! Jesus Christ, have this baby already so you can get your fucking hormones in check, will ya?"

With that Derek stormed out of the nursery, grabbing his car keys and cell phone off the entryway table and slamming the front door as he stomped out of the house.

Across the street Samantha was heading inside when she heard a loud noise coming from the Miller's house. She watched as Derek jumped into his truck and drove away. He didn't even glance in her direction. *What was that all about? Shit, he looked pissed,* Samantha thought. She grabbed her phone and went to send him a text message. She started to text: what is going on? You ok? She was about to hit send when something caught her attention. She slowly looked up at the house across the street and caught a glimpse of Elizabeth looking out the nursery window. She was looking in her direction and, if she was not mistaken, Samantha saw tears. All of a sudden she felt sick to her stomach. *Holy shit, she knows.*

CHAPTER TWENTY-ONE

Samantha had a hard time sleeping that night. She tossed and turned thinking of what to do. She played out all the possible scenarios in her mind. If Elizabeth knew, she would have confronted Samantha by now, she thought. Or was she waiting to get John alone and tell him. Either way, Sam knew she needed to get some sleep so she could face whatever was about to happen. At 1am., frustrated with not being able to sleep, Samantha got up and went into the bathroom to get a Xanax so she could calm down. When she returned to bed, John was on his phone typing away furiously. She looked at him puzzled. John looked up. "Sorry baby, did I wake you?" She shook her head. "It's the office. They're changing my itinerary for tomorrow." She wanted to ask him who was up at this time, changing itineraries? But she had more important things to worry about. She reached over and gave him a kiss on the cheek and rolled over and tried to sleep.

After a rough night of barely any sleep, John left for an early flight to Boston for business. A last minute time change for his business trip would normally have upset Samantha, but she was relieved after the blow up at the Miller's the day before as it gave her some alone time to think. She debated on telling her husband what she had seen but she knew he would tell her to mind her own business. Little did he know that it was Samantha's business and if she and Derek were found out, it would soon be all of their business. Both homes would never be the same and hearts would be broken.

Samantha waited anxiously for Elizabeth to leave for work. She kept peeking out the kitchen window to see if she had left yet. At 7am she started to panic that Elizabeth's car was still parked in their driveway. *Please leave, Elizabeth, Please. I need to know what is going on. I need to know if you know. I need your husband.* Finally at 7:10 she saw the black Escalade pull out of the driveway. Samantha let out a huge breath. She then ran to her phone. She starred at it for a minute wishing that Derek would contact her first so that she didn't have to. *What do I even say to him? So, I saw you drive off like a mad man yesterday, what's going on? Do I need to hire a divorce lawyer?* Still looking at her cell phone she said out loud, "You idiot, don't you know how to cover your tracks! *Men...*" Then she had second thoughts - *she* didn't want to tell him what she had seen. *Why open up a can of worms if I don't need to. Maybe they were arguing over what to eat for dinner.* But still, that look on Elizabeth's face was haunting Samantha. Something was wrong and she needed to find out what it was. She needed to prepare for damage control if needed. Although she was terrified to find out what was going on, she was also a little turned on by the excitement. The thought that Elizabeth might know made Samantha feel powerful and in control; she felt alive.

She threw caution to the wind and figured she would act normal. She waited until 7:25 then pulled up his name and hit 'dial'. After the first ring he answered.

"Hey! Hot stuff."

That's a good start. Maybe I was worried over nothing. "Why hello, Mr. Miller. How are you this morning?"

"Better now that you called," he replied in a low voice. Samantha was starting to feel frisky and knew exactly what to do.

"Glad to hear that, Mr. Miller. I wanted to call and let you know that you've just been enrolled in the obscene caller of the month club."

"Really, how did I get so lucky?"

Samantha chuckled into the phone. "Oh, you have no idea how lucky you are about to get, Mr. Miller." Sam then hit end on her phone and quickly opened up her text message icon and sent him a picture. She had been waiting to use this particular picture at just the right moment. She giggled and waited for her phone to ring, which she was sure would be any second. Instead she heard *ding ding*. She looked down at her phone and saw one reply from Derek Miller. She knew this was the moment of truth. Would he play or were they done? She opened the text message up and read:

FUCK YEAH SAMANTHA!!

She knew he wouldn't be able to resist her after the photo she had just sent of herself wearing a sexy black lace bra and panty set, thigh highs and heels. She replied:

You approve Mr. Miller?

Oh yes!! How long ago did you take this? Are you still wearing it?

I can be back in it within 5 minutes, want to play?

Well I can be over in less than 4 minutes. I'm so ready baby! Instant hard on!

That's what I want to hear. I'm about to start without you. You better get over here. Doors unlocked cowboy. Saddle up!

Samantha placed her phone down and dashed up to her bedroom. She quickly went in to her closet and grabbed her sexy ensemble. She put it on and then sat on the edge of her bed with her legs crossed, leaning back, which allowed her hair to cascade down her back and away from her neck. She looked up and Derek was standing in her doorway looking at her with lust in his eyes. She was breathtaking and no matter how many times they had been with each other he ached for her, it was never enough. It left him craving for more. He realized at that moment that he was falling and falling hard. He couldn't get enough of her. His fight with Elizabeth had escaped him. He wanted to tell Samantha what had transpired the day before but with just one look at her, he was putty. Something about this woman was making Derek crazy. Ever since she walked across the street and smiled at him he had wanted her. Right at this moment all he could think about was this beautiful woman in front of him that he was about to have. He walked over to the bed and started to caress her long legs over the thigh highs; he stopped at the high stiletto heels and grinned over at Samantha. "We can leave these on. Mmm, this just gets better and better." Derek sat down on the edge of the bed next to her and softly kissed her shoulder. "Baby, you are smoking hot."

"Mr. Miller, I believe you know exactly what buttons to push. Keep going."

"I want to take my time and kiss each part of your body, it's my wonderland," he answered as his lips trailed her collar bone.

"Take your time, hot stuff….it sure doesn't get better than this. Unless of course, I'm denied this pleasure like the other day."

Derek's body tensed and Samantha realized she had made a mistake. Lost in passion she wasn't paying attention to what she was saying. Obviously their fight had nothing to do with her otherwise he wouldn't be here in her bed. She could tell by Derek's reaction that she had hit a nerve. *Sam, let it go. You can ask about it afterwards. Ok, let me lighten the mood. Don't stop now, Derek. If I needed a quickie, I would have fucked my husband.*

"Mmm, Mr. Miller, I enjoy having my own little sex slave right across the street." She was trying to get him back in the game. But Derek was quiet, thinking of how to explain what had happened with his wife and how he was starting to have strong feelings towards Samantha. *She must have felt me tense up. Should I tell her what happened? I need to tell her that things are changing between us. I need to know if it's just me or if she feels it too.* He didn't want to stop pleasing her but he needed to talk to her. He wanted her to know that this wasn't just some fling. He paused for a minute, still running his hands up and down her legs. He looked up at her and looked into her green eyes and felt confident enough to speak. "Sam…"

"Hmm," Samantha looked over at him but before he could speak her house phone began to ring. She looked at the caller ID and didn't recognize the number. She sat up, forcing Derek to move off her and quickly grabbed the phone on the bedside table.

"Hello?"

"Hi, uh Sam, it's me, Lizzie, is Derek there? I tried him at home and on his cell, but no answer, I can't reach him and... AHHHHHH!" Elizabeth let out a painful cry.

Samantha sat up in bed pushing Derek to get up, mouthing to him that it was his wife and something was wrong.

"Elizabeth, are you ok?" Samantha asked while watching Derek. Derek stood at the side of the bed shaking his head and waving his hands that he wasn't there.

"I'm going into labor! Is he there? I need my husband, Sam!" Elizabeth was yelling in pain.

"Derek! Elizabeth is in labor!" He stood there for a brief second not sure what to do, but then he rushed out the bedroom door. "Tell her I'm on my way!"

Samantha sat on her bed alone. She knew she should feel happy that Elizabeth was about to have a baby, any friend would be, but Samantha wasn't just any friend and there was a part of her that was mad. She was mad at the woman for having a baby and mad that she had again ruined her 'coffee' time.

CHAPTER TWENTY-TWO

"Turn right!" Samantha ordered John as he turned his Mercedes into the hospital entrance. The building was always brightly lit and busy. She remembered coming here a few times over the past couple of years, always with such high hopes for the future. She was dreading coming back, knowing what memories she had here. This was the place where her dreams were taken from her. This was where her life had become such a dramatic whirlpool of loss. Not only once but twice, she had had to hear the doctor say, "I'm sorry, not this time Samantha." This is where she had been told to make a "fresh start."

Trying not to dwell on her past she was looking straight ahead at the sign that read deliveries. As John pulled into a parking space, she felt a buzz in her pocket. She pulled out her cell phone and saw that it was a text from Lauren. She felt more irritated than before. She had hoped it would have been from Derek. Dismissing the text from her best friend, Samantha didn't reply.

Instead she threw her phone into her handbag, hoping John didn't notice her frustration. The last thing she needed was to explain why she was in such a foul mood. Explaining to him that the last place she wanted to be was here was one thing but to tell him that her lover had not responded to her messages probably wouldn't go over too well.

Samantha's thoughts went to her neighbor. Even though she had Derek on the brain she wondered about Elizabeth. She liked Elizabeth enough. They occasionally went out together, and got along fairly well, but there were times she couldn't help but feel annoyed with her. She was always so happy, sweet, and too perky…God, what did Derek see in her?

Again she felt the buzz of her cell phone going off in her handbag. Hoping it was a text from Derek she quickly looked at it, Lauren, again. Samantha could feel the anger building up inside her. Why wasn't Derek contacting her? All she needed was a hello, I'm thinking of you, something to let her know that she was on his mind. Deep down she knew she was being unrealistic, after all the man was about to become a daddy. But Samantha needed reassuring that this baby wouldn't come between them. Answer me, goddamn it. Just then her phone went off again. This had to be Derek, it had to be. But as soon as she looked down she noticed it was her best friend. For fuck's sake, she thought, what does Lauren want? Whatever it is it can wait. Frustrated and annoyed she turned her phone off and flung it back into her purse. No more false hopes, she thought. Anyway, you'll be face to face with him any minute. He'll no choice but to answer for his silence.

She took one last peek of herself in the visor mirror. John was going on about something. All she heard was "trip," "Boston," "a few nights." Same old story, she nodded at her husband as if to say sure, whatever. *Have fun John* she thought and rolled her eyes.

Dr. Elizabeth Miller, PHD…boring…Samantha's thoughts went back to Elizabeth. Maybe Derek liked woman with titles. Keep your title, fancy pants. Hubby sure doesn't mind being bossed around in the bedroom. In fact he begs for it. He wants a woman in control not a wimpy little girl. You see, Elizabeth, one thing you are missing is power, that's what I have. Or had.

Walking into the entrance of the hospital Samantha's nerves started to get the better of her. She wasn't sure if she was feeling uneasy about being at the hospital, or if she was angry at being ignored by her lover. Either way she was not in a good place.

Samantha knew how to fake her way through being at the hospital. She knew how to keep her emotions in check. She was a pro at that. But not having spoken to Derek was another thing. They had not spoken since yesterday's little rendezvous. And he hadn't returned her calls or text messages. The more time passed without a word from Derek the more she became annoyed with him. The more she allowed herself to think about his silence, the more neglected she felt. Samantha Bennett did not deal with neglect well at all.

"I know where we're going, Sam, stop pulling on me! The baby isn't going anywhere." Samantha hadn't realized she was tugging on his arm.

"Sorry, John. Just a little anxious I guess." Samantha apologized, trying to remember that he had made it home just in time to catch the last visiting hour at the hospital. The poor guy had barely had time to change and grab a granola bar. Still Samantha couldn't care less about her husband's needs; she was more concerned with getting up to the Miller's room, mainly to see Derek.

"I'm sorry too, I'm just tired." John replied.

As they walked hand in hand towards the automatic doors, they followed the signs towards the maternity ward on the fifth floor. Samantha barely took note of his bad mood, with her own thoughts consuming her.

While waiting for the elevator she couldn't stop thinking about Derek and how he would react to seeing her here. John was too busy texting on his phone to even try and carry a conversation anyway.

Things had been moving along, and Derek was a fantastic lay, but something had been gnawing at her. She loved the attention he gave her, but she had started to question their affair. While fooling around yesterday, she knew he wanted to say something to her. At first she thought it was about the Miller's fight, but after playing the scene in her head, his eyes were too telling. She knew he was going to tell her something that would have changed their relationship. Samantha was not about to have that happen. She wanted a distraction not another husband. He obviously was moving in another direction, and not the one Samantha had anticipated. *Please don't make a stupid mistake. If you were going to say what I think you were ...I will have to say goodbye, again.*

Samantha couldn't help but fidget with the baby gift bag and balloon, while waiting for the damn door to open. John stood behind her with his hands on her shoulders, rubbing them. "You ok?" he whispered.

"Yeah, I'll be ok." *Now you ask? Go back to your phone, John, really its ok. What you don't know won't hurt you.*

The elevator ride to the maternity ward seemed to take forever. She and John stood in silence. She wondered if he was thinking about their loss. Was he just as torn up inside as she was? Then again, he hadn't put his phone down long enough to notice the tears in her eyes. Samantha fought them back and took a deep breath.

They had finally arrived at the maternity floor. They were buzzed inside and walked towards the Miller's room. Samantha had to fight back the tears when she heard the cries of the babies, seeing proud parents, grandparents, small children running around wearing big brother/big sister t-shirts. Luckily Elizabeth's room was right around the corner and she didn't have to have it thrown in her face for too long; she didn't know how much more she could handle.

"Knock Knock," John said as he stuck his head inside the room, with his wife in tow.

"Hey." Derek pulled the door open all the way and looked past John and immediately looked at Samantha. "Thanks for coming," he said as he shook John's hand and gave him a pat on the back,

"Congrats, man," said John.

Derek walked over to Samantha and kissed her on the cheek. Samantha felt uncomfortable; Derek did seem happy to see her, but then why ignore her calls and texts? She turned her attention to Elizabeth.

"Congrats, how are you feeling, Elizabeth?" Samantha walked over to the bed where Elizabeth sat taking a sip of her ginger ale. "Wow, you're lucky you have your own room, I guess working for the hospital has its perks." She placed the gift bag and balloons on the chair in the corner. Elizabeth gave a polite smile and nodded to say thanks. Something was off and Samantha felt it.

"Hey, you want to see him?" Derek asked, with a big ear to ear grin.

"Of course, lead the way."

Derek leaned down and kissed his wife on the head. "Want to take a walk with us?"

"No, I'm a little tired. I'll wait here."

Derek headed out with John and Samantha beside him. Walking around the corner they reached the nursery where all the babies were lined up in their little plastic bassinets swaddled in blankets and wearing little crochets hats. Proud parents and friends and family of all the newborns hovered around the glass staring in. Derek scooted his way through towards the end where Baby DJ lay peacefully sleeping, wearing a blue knitted hat with a small stuffed baseball placed in the corner of his makeshift crib.

"He's adorable, man." John patted Derek on the back then placed his arm around Samantha's shoulder. Derek watched his son through the glass in amazement. He looked just like all the other proud fathers watching their newborn babies.

Samantha couldn't help but feel a twinge of jealousy that he wasn't looking at her. She knew she was being silly and selfish, but she didn't care. John's phone vibrated. He looked down at the message. "I'm going to find a restroom, got to hit the head." They both watched as John headed down the hall.

"So." Derek grinned at Samantha.

"He's beautiful." Samantha fought back the tears that were forming in full force.

"Thanks, it's an amazing feeling. I just can't believe he's mine. He's my son."

She looked up to find Derek staring at her. "I'm sorry, I didn't mean to go on like that, you alright?"

"Oh, don't be sorry, you should be excited. I just…." Sam wanted to open up to her lover, but she knew once she started she wouldn't be able to stop. Besides, she gave him her body, she was not about to give him her soul. He was already on the verge of messing this up; she didn't want to fuel the fire. She took a deep breath and looked at the babies. She and Derek were standing side by side and she knew he wanted to say something. Just as she was about to excuse herself to the ladies room he whispered in her ear, "I'm sorry about yesterday."

"Are you?" Samantha couldn't help the sarcasm in her voice. She was annoyed and wanted answers.

"Of course I am. Sam, what's going on? I have been a little preoccupied in case you hadn't noticed." Samantha could feel the tension in his voice but she wanted him to know how disappointed she was with him.

"Oh, I know you have been preoccupied, Derek. But I was beginning to feel like yesterday's trash being ignored and all! It takes two second to answer a text, Derek. Surely, you had two seconds to spare for me. You know, your lover?" Samantha turned, facing him, making sure he saw how upset she was.

"What? Come on, Sam, that's not fair. My wife just had our baby. You looked fucking amazing and if Lizzie hadn't been in labor, then we would have spent all day in that bed." He reached over and squeezed her arm. "Trust me, you are on my mind everyday all day. But give me a break this one time. I promise I will make it up to you."

With just his touch Samantha started to cave in. She also didn't want to waste anymore stolen moments fighting with him. She laughed to lighten the mood, and just hearing him say how good she looked gave her confidence again. Satisfied with his reaction, she wanted him. She also wanted to make sure that he wanted her and only her. "Every day all day, huh?" she teased. "You could have responded to at least one of my messages. You will pay for that, Mr. Miller."

"Oh, I'm sure I will. And I look forward to it. Sam, I was hoping to chat yesterday, you know that, but things didn't work out as I planned." Derek rubbed the side of her arm.

"Oh. Well maybe tomorrow before you pick up Elizabeth?" A couple walked by and forced Samantha to move closer to Derek.

Being this close to him radiated heat throughout her body. She needed to feel his body against her at this very moment.

"I don't know, I'm not sure what time she'll be discharged. I'll text when I get a free moment." Derek smiled. "I promise."

"Promises, promises…." Samantha flirted back, still needing reassurance. "Derek, is everything alright? Are we good, nothing changed, right?"

"Absolutely, couldn't be better!"

"Well then maybe I could persuade you to join me in the janitor's closet over there for a quickie." Samantha joked.

Derek raised his eye brows in amusement at Samantha's comment. Before he could respond the bell rang and the nurse's voice came through the speakers overhead announcing that visiting hours would be ending within the next fifteen minutes. They both noticed John making his way back to the nursery glass just in time to walk back with them to Elizabeth's room to say good night.

No one noticed Elizabeth standing at the end of the hallway watching.

CHAPTER TWENTY-THREE

Ok, Derek, now would be the perfect time to call me. Doesn't he realize this may be our last chance for any alone time? Doesn't he realize that the baby is going to consume all of his time? Samantha snatched her cell phone from the kitchen counter and debated whether she should just call him. On one hand she really wasn't in the mood to deal with him this early, or face what she already suspected their conversation to be. However, she couldn't handle this feeling of being pushed aside. She always came second to John, she was not about to become second to her lover. He hadn't left for the hospital yet so why not call? Samantha knew by the way Derek had acted the past few times they were together that he was no longer a casual lover; he was starting to act like a husband. One is enough, she thought to herself as she rolled her eyes. Sure she wanted him to want her but she had no intentions of him loving her. That was not part of the game. However, now that his attention was elsewhere she found herself constantly thinking about him. She knew she should just wait for him to contact her, but she wasn't used to being ignored by him and it bothered her. "Oh, let me just call him."

Samantha took a deep breath in and let it out trying to sound as if everything was normal. "Good Morning."

"Hey, hot stuff, how are you?" Samantha breathed a sigh of relief when he answered, but could detect a different tone in his voice. Usually he spoke with a confidence which normally turned her on, but there was no trace of that this morning.

He cleared his throat. "I was just about to head out to pick up Lizzie and the baby from the hospital."

"Oh yea, I actually have plans to meet the girls soon, but I thought I would call and see what's going on." Samantha gathered her purse and keys and stood by the front door staring at the Miller's house.

"Sorry, Sam, but I'm actually kind of late as it is. I still have to stop at the post office and then get coffee for Lizzie. I really want to talk to you, but now is not the time. I'll text you later on." Derek hung up the phone while walking out the front door.

Samantha was left stunned for a minute; she couldn't understand what had just happened. Derek had never blown her off before, why the sudden change? She stood there frozen. Derek was practically running to his truck as if he was being chased. He hopped in and reversed down the driveway without even looking in the rear view, without even looking in her direction. *What the fuck, what is going on?* Samantha didn't have to wait for their chat, she had a feeling she knew what he would say, but the fact that he wasn't paying attention to her made her feel angry.

Coffee for the queen, huh? Of course he would go to the post office first since it was two blocks before Starbucks. *I don't have too much time to spare before meeting the girls, but I didn't say where I was meeting them.* And as luck would have it she was meeting them at the diner right next door to Starbucks. *Making him face me so I can see what was going on would ease my anxiety. I mean, how could he go from hot too cold in a matter of one night? It was just yesterday at the hospital he was touching my arm and telling me how he wanted me and thought about me every day. Now he's running out the door without a text or call or a quick kiss? Screw you, Derek.* She locked up and headed out as quickly as she could. She was determined to beat him to the coffee shop.

Samantha pulled into the parking lot of Starbucks and parked her Audi R7. She put the car in park and scanned the small parking lot and didn't see his car. Good, she thought, he wasn't there yet. She had ran out of her house so quick she had very little time to freshen up. While watching the entrance to the parking lot she frantically felt around for her lip gloss in her purse. Samantha knew she needed to calm down so she wouldn't cause any suspicion. She had to admit that she felt a little silly for stalking her lover but she knew she needed to see him. All she wanted was some reassurance from him. She just wanted Derek and she missed his touch. If this were a week ago, she would be with him in her bed, enjoying him. Now she was alone, again. Samantha pulled out her lip gloss and was looking in the mirror to apply a fresh coat when she recognized him. She dropped the gloss and turned the visor to make sure she wouldn't miss him. *You can do this. Act cool.* Taking a deep breath she waited for him to step out of his car.

Samantha shut her car door and was pretending to look in her purse for something when she heard Derek behind her. "Hey, what are you doing here?" Derek asked.

"Well, if you must know I'm meeting the girls for coffee. What are you doing here? Shouldn't you be getting your wife and baby?"

"I am. I thought I told you I had to run an errand and then grab coffee. You didn't mention you were coming here. Samantha Bennett, are you stalking me?" Derek teased.

"Like I said, I'm meeting the girls for coffee. I didn't know I had to tell you about my whereabouts. And no, I'm not stalking you, but I did see you run out of the house like it was on fire! Lizzie must really want coffee." Samantha couldn't control the sarcasm in her voice.

"Sam, I was supposed to be at the hospital twenty minutes ago. I really have to go, I'm sorry, really I am. I promise though I'll text you when it's a good time to chat." Derek reached over to touch her arm, but she took a step back.

Samantha stood there staring at her lover, trying to control her anger. She had that feeling again in the pit of her stomach. The feeling of being blown off and she didn't like it. She had never experienced it as much as she had with Derek in the past three days. "Ok, well my friends will be here any minute if they're not already inside. I won't keep you any longer!"

"Sam, don't be like that…" Just as he was about to reach out to her again his phone chimed. "I'm sorry, Sam, they're waiting for me. Lizzie is blowing up my phone. I can't even go in to buy coffee now. I have to go. Please try and understand. Give me a break. I am trying my best here."

"I get it, Derek, loud and clear. You don't have time for me, its fine, really." She furrowed her brow and turned on her heels to leave.

"Sam…" Derek called out to her but she kept on walking.

A small sense of satisfaction fell over Samantha, knowing he was standing there feeling lousy, most likely leaving him in a mood. Now go get your wife, she laughed to herself. She went inside and waited for Derek to leave before driving next door to meet her friends.

"Hey, doll" Lauren said as she slid into the booth across from Samantha "I just saw hot Derek."

Shit. Samantha shook her head and shrugged her shoulders. "Oh, really? You saw him just now?" *Oh great, did she see us? I'll never hear the fucking end of it.* Acting as if nothing was out of the ordinary Samantha read the menu, nervously waiting for her response. Lauren shook her head and continued to speak while they waited for the waitress.

"I saw him on Starlight Path at the light. I waved but I don't think he was paying any attention to anything around him. He looked a little upset. He's a nice piece of ass but boy he looked a little freaky. Sam, you always have the weirdest neighbors. My God, what is in that house that causes your 'friends' to go nuts? The last ones leave overnight and this one is just all, I don't know, too tightly wound up. Remind me to never move onto your street," Lauren laughed. "Oh, well, I see Christie is running late."

Samantha just stared at the menu, trying not to let her friend see that she was crazed with how things had been left with Derek. She also felt good though, knowing that he left looking upset.

"Why is that girl always late?"

Thank God she hadn't seen them together, Lauren would have had a million questions and with the way Samantha felt right now, it was better this way. Although she felt proud that she'd made him feel like shit, she couldn't help but feel a bit vulnerable at the moment. Lauren wouldn't understand her affair, nor would she approve. Wild and free as she may be, Lauren was faithful. Lauren had also never experienced loss like Samantha had.

"Oh, I forgot to ask you if you would mind if I cancelled our girl's night out. One of the guys from the bank asked me out; he's been asking for some time now so I figured why not, right? But I know this could be trouble, ya know, don't shit where you eat and all, but he's super cute so who knows?"

Samantha, distracted by her own thoughts of what had just transpired with Derek, hadn't even noticed Lauren was still talking. She started to feel as if the ground was opening up and was about to swallow her whole. Her conversation with Derek was enough but there was something else that made her feel uneasy. Then it hit her. Lauren had mentioned the old neighbors. All of a sudden she started to feel dizzy.

"Hello, earth to Sam!" Lauren waved her hand in front of Samantha's face. "You alright, girl? You seem out of it."

"Oh yeah, I'm good. Hey can you order me a coffee? I just want to run to the bathroom." Samantha slid out of the booth and headed towards the restrooms.

"Sure, go ahead"

Samantha could feel her heart beating a mile a minute. *What the fuck is wrong with me? What am I doing?* She looked at herself in the mirror, dabbing a cold wet paper towel under her eyes; she didn't know if she should laugh or cry. She had never acted this way before with anyone. So why Derek? What was so special about him?

Someone knocked on the bathroom door. "I'll be right out." Samantha took a deep breath and glanced in the mirror. *It's not you, Sam, it's them. Calm down. You know what needs to be done.* Finally gaining her composure, she headed out to drink her coffee and make the most of this time with her friends.

CHAPTER TWENTY-FOUR

"DAMN IT!" Derek exclaimed. Think, Derek, think. He had been sitting at his desk staring at a blank computer screen for hours; frustrated, confused, lost and lonely. He hadn't been able to type a single word except for 'Sam,' over and over he had typed her name. Why? For starters he couldn't stop thinking about their last conversation at Starbucks, though that had been almost two weeks ago. Second, he was hiding out to keep his wife from nagging him about not getting anything accomplished. Derek loved being home with his son. He loved feeding him and watching him sleep. He would lay on the couch with the baby resting on his chest. It was the greatest feeling, but something felt like it was missing. He couldn't think straight. He knew they should be spending this time together as a family, and that he needed to be a better husband, but his thoughts were consumed with Samantha. That's what was missing...

Samantha. He wanted to know what she was doing, and what she was thinking. Most importantly, what was she feeling?

Derek would feed the baby in his office or rock him to sleep, so he could stare out of his window hoping to catch a glimpse of her. He knew he couldn't run over to her if he saw her. Elizabeth had them on lock down. Once they came home from the hospital she became his warden; he was forbidden to go anywhere except to his office and even then she would pop in and ask, "Where are you in your great American novel?" There was obviously something going on with his wife but he was too tired and too consumed with his son and lover to ask, or to care. He had decided it was best to keep his mouth shut and to stay away from her and her moods. Eventually things would go back to normal and he could get his life back, right?

He tried sending Samantha a few text messages, even emails, but she would barely respond. Every answer was short.

Derek found himself daydreaming about her; the way she smiled when he kissed the inside of her neck or how she always smelled of warm vanilla sugar. The way the curve of her body felt when he touched her. He wanted her to be in his arms again. He needed her. But what was worse was that he wanted her to need him. He was a sensible guy, always had his head on straight, did the right thing, but now it was if he had no control. *I can't let her walk away, not after everything we shared together. If only I could see her and explain what I feel…I know she feels it too. She knows this is a huge adjustment with having Lizzie home and a new baby; maybe she's giving ME space? Jesus, Sam,*

188

I didn't ask for space. Derek heard a loud noise. *Shit, here we go again. The warden must be pissed at something.*

"What's going on in here?" Derek cautiously entered the nursery. Little DJ was crying in his crib as Elizabeth slammed things down on the changing table. Derek just stood there, scratching the back of his head.

"Derek, how many times do I have to tell you to close the damn wipe case? If you leave it open, they dry out! And they aren't cheap!" Sensing her frustration, Derek stood there biting his tongue. The last thing he wanted was to aggravate the situation any further. He told himself that it had to be anxiety. After all, she was a new mommy, she had every right to feel overwhelmed. Derek just wasn't too sure about how to keep his own emotions in check.

Ignoring her commentary on the wipe situation, Derek spoke calmly, trying not to enrage her anymore. "Lizzie, you want me to change him?"

"No, I can manage, but it would be nice if you could get a bottle warmed up, he's ready to eat." Her back was still turned to him. Derek wanted to reach to her to hold her and let her know that he was there to help and to reassure her that she was doing a great job. But he knew his wife too well. He knew now would not be the time to try and coddle her, she would only feel resentment and would likely lash out.

Shaking his head in bewilderment, he turned and walked out of the nursery to retrieve the bottle. As he was putting the bottle in the bottle warmer, he couldn't help but think that there was more to the great wipe saga. He knew that something had been bothering her since they had been home from the hospital; she would only speak to him when she needed to, and even then she would keep it short and cold. It had taken everything inside him to ignore her comment about the wipes. He just didn't want to get into it over fucking wipes. Elizabeth was normally a very strong woman but there was something not right. This was not the same woman he had married; sure she was tough, she had to be to do the job she did. But this person was cold and indifferent.

"Derek! Could you please move a little faster with the bottle! It's not rocket science! It's already mixed, what is taking you so long? Put the damn thing in the warmer and press the button!" He heard more not so pleasant demands but tuned them out. *Here we go again*, he thought to himself as he grabbed the bottle from the warmer.

Derek walked back up to the nursery; Elizabeth looked as though she was trying to remain calm. He took the baby from his wife's arms and started to feed him in the rocker. "Why don't you go lie down for a bit, I'll feed him and put him down for a nap." Derek looked up at Elizabeth who nodded and started to walk out of the nursery. Just as she was almost out of the room, Derek asked, "Is something wrong?" She took a deep breath and slowly turned around to face her husband with rage in her eyes. She stood frozen for a moment, as if not sure what to do or say, but before she could stop herself the words came flying out of her mouth.

"I saw you."

Derek could see the rage seething from her eyes. He had no idea what she was talking about.

"You saw me? What do you mean?"

Elizabeth looked at her husband dead in the eyes, "I saw you. I saw you both."

"Ok…am I missing something? You saw me and who?"

"You know who." Tears began to run down Elizabeth's face.

"No, I don't and this is ridiculous. What is going on? Lizzie, please talk to me. What is going on? What did you see?"

"You can't deny it, Derek. I know what I saw. At first I thought there was no way but now it makes sense."

"Deny what? I don't even know what I did! Who exactly did you see me with?"

Elizabeth knew there was no turning back now. She took a deep breath, wiped her eyes, looked at her husband and calmly said, "Sam."

Derek sat there puzzled. He hadn't seen Samantha in weeks. What was she talking about? He rolled his eyes and chuckled. "This again? Seriously Lizzie, didn't we have this conversation already?" Derek had finished feeding the baby; he held DJ on his knee cupping the baby's chin with one hand while using the other to rub and pat his back. DJ burped. "Atta boy!" Derek removed the baby's bib and placed him in the crib for his nap. Once the baby was nicely tucked in, he motioned his wife to the door by putting his arm around her shoulder, trying to console her. He escorted her out of the nursery and closed the door behind them; she pushed his arm away. "Let's start at the beginning. What did Sam and I do now Lizzie? What crime

191

did we commit? Please tell me so we can end this obsession with her once and for all." Derek was trying not to lose his cool with Elizabeth but he honestly had no idea what she could have seen to cause such friction. Elizabeth walked past him and went straight into their bedroom. She turned around to face her husband. He knew she was about to lose it. All the emotions of the past weeks flew out of her mouth.

"I don't know, I don't know, Derek!" Elizabeth covered her face with her hands. Tears were falling in full force. Her shoulders shook with each sob. "Something is wrong. I've have been trying to deal with it on my own and keep telling myself that maybe I'm just overly sensitive, and tired, b-but I can't shake it. Seeing you with her, the way you held her arm and the look… the way you looked at her. That's how you used to look at me. I can't erase that image. I know what I saw!"

Derek was losing his patience with her. "When did I touch Sam? I'm a little confused here. I've been here with you and the baby. You're not making any sense. I'm totally lost. Clearly you're delusional."

"Don't you dare insult me!" She stormed past Derek and ran downstairs to the kitchen. Derek was confused. Clearly his wife thought she had seen something happen between him and Samantha but when? *Shit, when was the last time I was with Sam, think man.* He went down to the kitchen, anticipating a fight with his wife but trying to recall the last time he had seen Samantha. *The hospital! But all we did was watch the newborns.* As if smacked by his own hand, it hit him… *The babies. I touched her arm to console her, that's all. It's not as if we were all over each other. Jesus Christ, all these months being careful and a fucking touch on her arm…*

Elizabeth was making coffee. When she saw him she quickly turned her back to him again. Derek took a seat at the table. "Lizzie, I'm not trying to insult you. I'm trying to understand what you think you saw and when."

"What I *think* I saw? Really, Derek? Don't play dumb." She scurried around the kitchen pouring water into the coffee maker and scooping the grinds into the paper filter.

"Enlighten me, Lizzie. When did this happen? What cardinal sin did Sam and I commit?" Derek slapped his palms down on the table, no longer able to hide his frustration.

Elizabeth grabbed a mug from the cabinet and slammed the door.

"At the hospital. You really should be more observant, Derek. I decided to join you. Boy was I surprised when I came around the corner and saw you standing there with her all cozy by the nursery window. You were touching her arm! It was as if you two were the only people on earth! You looked at her the way a lion looks before he pounces on his prey. It's very evident that *my* husband is messing around! You are not *just* having coffee with the neighbor, as you call it. I can't begin to explain what I am feeling right now Derek. How could you? How could you do this to me? To your child? And with her?"

"Lizzie, I'm not having this argument with you again; I don't know what you *thought* you saw but it was nothing more than a friend consoling another friend. Have you forgotten that she has lost a baby? Twice? Surely you're not that unsympathetic to another woman's loss? Could you imagine what she went through?" He decided to take a softer approach with his wife. He knew she was emotional and over-tired and he needed to defuse the situation. *This has to stop and now. I thought we were past this; I really don't have time for this shit.* He got up from the table and walked over to his wife, enveloping her in his arms; he brushed the hair away from her face and rubbed the wet tear streaks from her cheeks. Her big brown eyes looked up at him and he saw the vulnerability. "I love you, Lizzie, you just gave birth to our beautiful baby boy. You are tired; your body is adjusting to all the hormones. Please, don't do this to yourself. There is nothing going on between Sam and me besides friendship. There is nothing inappropriate going on, except sharing the same sugar spoon. I touched her arm, no big deal. Now if you saw me doing this ..." He reached down and slowly kissed her lips. She just looked at him with a sheepish grin. He knew it was working. "Please baby, tell me what do I have to do or say to make you believe me?"

"Derek?" He looked down at her with questioning eyes. "I think I'm going to take the baby to my sisters for a couple of days. You know, just to get away. Lori and my parents can help me with the baby and I can get some rest. Maybe you're right, maybe I just need time to relax. I know I have been all over the place these days. I just feel so overwhelmed and like something is off. My sister can help and I can get some rest. I haven't had a break at all. Maybe I shouldn't have worked to the last minute. But I know with a little separation and some rest things will be better. Plus, with me and the baby gone you can work on your book without any interruptions. I think some distance will be good for us."

Derek could see how upset she was and how much she needed this. *Maybe now, I can talk to Sam and settle this once and for all,* he thought. He smiled at his wife. "Whatever you need, baby. If you think this is best then go. I will miss you and our little guy. But, you promise only a couple of days. I don't know what I would do without you both." And with that he kissed her cheek and walked out of the kitchen, heading up to his office.

Elizabeth stood there sipping her coffee. She wanted to trust her husband. She wanted to believe that there was nothing going on besides an innocent friendship, but something was nagging at her, something he had said. No matter how hard she tried to believe him, she couldn't help but feel like something wasn't adding up. Then like a lightning bolt it hit her. Her stomach turned and she held onto the kitchen counter for support. Her world started to close in. *Since when does Derek call me 'baby'?*

CHAPTER TWENTY-FIVE

After stalking Derek at Starbucks, Samantha kept her distance. She didn't want to but knew she needed to. Although she was hurting, she stayed on her side of the street. She felt bad about not going to see the baby once he was home, but she couldn't. She wanted to but she just couldn't. After DJ had been born she felt so alone, so lost. Nightmares of babies crying consumed her sleep. Every time she would go to them they were gone, but she could still hear their cries. She would search and search for them, up and down strange hallways for what seemed to be hours until the crying stopped. The silence always plunged her from sleep into the dark hours of night, sobbing. She would reach for John for comfort but he was hardly ever there. He was going on more and more business trips and Sam was feeling more and more alone. Samantha needed something to fill the void in her life. But Derek was making things so complicated. It was too hard. It wasn't supposed to be like this. Sure he had texted, emailed, messaged her almost daily since the encounter at Starbucks, but she barely responded. She needed to talk to him but she wasn't ready to cut ties, not yet, not while John was so distracted with work. John, she needed her husband more than ever. She needed him to hold her and let her know that everything was going to be alright, she needed to tell him her feelings and she needed to tell him now. Samantha was on her way up to the bedroom to talk to him when he yelled out to her.

"Hey, Sam, did you pick up my suit from the cleaners?"

"What? I didn't hear you from downstairs," Samantha answered as she strolled into their bedroom.

Immediately she noticed the luggage open on top of their bed. John was carrying clothing and shoes from the closet. She felt a knot inside of her stomach begin to turn. *No, not now, please don't leave me...* She wanted to yell to him but the words wouldn't come out.

"My suit, from the cleaners?" He looked at her, waiting for her to answer.

"Huh? What's this?"

"I'm leaving in a few hours on the red eye for a business trip; did you get my suit from the cleaners, Sam?'

"Yes, it's on the right hand side behind your garment bag. You didn't tell me you were leaving tonight."

"Sam, I told you weeks ago. I'm not sure how long I'll be this time, probably only a few days, a week tops." He grabbed the suit from the closet and laid it on the bed. "I'll let you know once I get there."

Samantha couldn't help but feel as though she was being abandoned. "I don't remember you telling me you were leaving again. You didn't mention it at dinner last night."

"Sam, I told you I had a trip coming up. Lately it's like talking to the wall."

"Don't go!" She sat down on the corner of the bed, staring at John's back. She felt the tears begin to form behind her lids, but refused to let them fall.

"John, is this trip really necessary? Can you postpone it? I wanted to talk to you." Her voice was shaky, on the verge of cracking. *Please don't cry* she thought to herself. *Why can't he see that I'm in pain? What happened to us being in sync? He used to know when I needed him. This isn't like him. This isn't my husband.*

"YES! It's necessary, it's business! What's with all the questions? You know I have to go on these trips. How do you think the bills get paid, Sam?" Samantha knew only too well from his tone that he didn't want to be bothered, but she needed to try and keep him here with her.

"John, please. Can't you just stay home this one time? Can't you get someone else to go? I just…I don't want to be alone. The nightmares are starting again, I feel so…" she let her words trail off as her eyes filled with tears and she couldn't hide them anymore. Surely after hearing about her nightmares he wouldn't leave. She felt so vulnerable. She was desperate to get his attention to keep him here. "Do you ever think about our baby girl?" He didn't respond; he kept packing as if on autopilot, his back to her, no emotion, nothing. "You know, she would be almost a year old now." She knew he had heard her, what she wasn't expecting was his reaction.

John stopped short and looked over at Samantha, he furrowed his brows. "What? We've been through this. I can't do this now. Not now Sam, I don't have time for this again." John continued to pack.

Trying to keep her emotions in check and not caring that John was in no mood to listen, she went on. "Don't you miss her? Why was she taken from me…US?" she cried out. She was desperate to make him listen. She didn't want to hurt anymore; she needed to make him understand how much she needed him. John marched over to her; any patience he replaced with an irritation which he no longer hid.

"DON'T! I'm not doing this again, Samantha. She was never ours! We *never* had her! I have a very important day tomorrow and I can't discuss this now. Why do you do this to me all the time? The car will be here soon to take me to the airport. Why do you keep dwelling on the past? I'm sorry about the nightmares but…Jesus, Sam, it's over, can't you let go? Make peace, I did." He started to turn his back to her when Samantha jumped up off the bed and grabbed his arm to pull him around. Now he was facing her and she wasn't going to hide her anger from him. She had had enough

"Oh, I'm sorry to inconvenience you! Next time I'll make an appointment with your secretary! Excuse me for having feelings and trying to discuss them with my husband….*sue me*!" She was livid with him, herself, the shit end of the stick she'd been given. She was going to make him listen to her and face the consequences afterwards. "How can you be so cold? Don't you wonder what our lives would have been like? What our little girl would look like? It's so quiet here in this house. It's deafening; there should be children's laughter and dirty finger prints on our walls…there should be more to life than this."

John just looked at her. Silent. She couldn't see anything in his normally beautiful eyes. They were vacant; she wasn't getting through to him. Her blood started to boil. "You seem to have forgotten you have a life, you wake up every morning with a purpose, a fancy job in the city, people rely on you, and then you get to come home to a wife who cooks and cleans and picks up your frigging dry clean! What about me? Day in, day out, I'm stuck here in these four walls all day! Alone! Don't you think it gets lonely? The highlight of my day is waiting for you to call and say let's go to dinner. It means changing out of my yoga pants and getting dressed up, Woohoo!" She was becoming unglued and there was no stopping her. She was barely making sense, jumping from one thought to another but she needed to release it. "Do you know that I sit here all day thinking about that god awful day? I was so afraid. Do you have any idea what it was like, having to deliver my baby so early not knowing if she would even make it? How could you? You weren't the one hooked up to machines and IV drips, being poked and prodded, nurses looking at you as though you were the one dying.

"When Alexa was born, my heart stopped. It was like an out of body experience, it didn't feel real. I saw her open her eyes, and take a shallow breath, I had a little glimmer of hope, but I knew…I knew she wouldn't last more than a few hours in

NICU, if she even made it out of the delivery room. My sweet innocent baby girl, she didn't have a chance and WHY? It's not fair John! I want my baby girl!"

"I want a life! I want the pain to stop! The nightmares to stop! The baby crying in my thoughts to stop!" Her tears were falling so hard, she was losing all control and all she saw were two dead eyes looking back at her. "I can't believe you, John. Here I am crying, telling you how I feel and you're too busy for me, you don't have time for me anymore! You aren't here half the time. I can't do this alone. Why can't you see that I need YOU?" She stopped, waiting for him to break down, grab her and hold her in his arms. Instead he took two steps backwards away from her, ran his fingers through his hair and placed his hands on his hips. This man in front of her was a stranger. This man was cold and unfeeling. For the first time in their relationship, Samantha was scared for their marriage.

"Samantha, I am not going to stand here and let you self-destruct. I am not going to allow you to blame me for your unhappiness. This is not my fault. Join a club, take up a hobby, read a book! Last time I checked you don't have to stay at home. You can go find a job! Join the human race again. For Christ sake, go back to work for all I care! But don't blame me for your boredom! I will not be your escape for not wanting to better yourself. And I have to work! Who do you think is paying for your designer handbags, your spa days? Your coffee dates? That would be me! I'm the one busting my ass for you! Stop and think about someone besides yourself! You're acting like a brat! And please, for the love of God; stop bringing up what we never had! It's horrible, I know, but I'm not discussing that day anymore!" He glared at her.

John's phone chirped: he glanced at the screen and scrolled through to read the message. Samantha jumped at him, grabbed his phone from his hands and flung it across the room. It landed on the rug with a thud.

"DAMMIT!" Her eyes were red and soaked with tears, her hands balled in fists at her sides. She was tired of always being second to his job.

John stopped and just stared in disbelief. "What the fuck, Samantha? Have you completely lost it? That was important." He paused and watched her for a few moments. "Do you need to speak with Dr. Meltzer again? I really think you should. Make an appointment today! I can't take this anymore. I have so much stress from everywhere! But what would you know? You want to blame anyone but yourself for your lack of a 'life'! It's not fair to put the blame on ME," He bent down to pick up his phone off the floor.

"FAIR, you wanna talk about fair? You are not the one who has to pee on sticks every month hoping to see two lines, but there never is. I have to keep track of when I'm ovulating so we hit at the right time…there is only that small window of opportunity and if you miss it, well then that's another month wasted. Finally I'm pregnant again, we were blessed. But wait, Sam's uterus is apparently a hostile womb, two miscarriages within months of each other. Do you have *any* idea what that was like, John? I couldn't protect my baby. I'm the one that felt her move and kick and grow inside me…NOT YOU! I don't need to talk to Dr. Meltzer; I don't need to be told to start fresh, if I hear fresh start one more time I think I'll go crazy!"

Her body was trembling and her breaths came short as she gasped for air. She cried rivers of tears, her eyes swollen and bloodshot, her face was covered in blotches, snot running out of her nose and she didn't care. It was now or never to unleash all this built-up anger and frustration at the hand she had been dealt. She didn't care if her husband wanted to hear it or not.

Sam felt John's eyes on her. She knew he loved her, and she desperately wanted him to hold her. He put his phone down and wrapped his arms around her. "I know it wasn't fair. I know it's been hard, with your dad leaving, losing your mom and then the miscarriages."

Samantha's breathing began to steady, and John felt her body relax in his arms. "I'm sorry, Sam. I really am, I shouldn't have jumped all over you like that. I guess I figured you were finally getting better and were beginning to accept what happened. I guess I was being an insensitive prick. I don't blame you for being upset with me. I love you. I want you to be happy. But you need to find your own happiness and not rely on me. I am here for you always; you know that don't you? And I promise when I get back we'll go somewhere alone together with no distractions. How does that sound? We'll have a fresh start. But right now I need to finish packing, I need to go on this trip."

Samantha pushed out of his arms, and brushed the hair away from her face, she saw it in his eyes. She had lost, again. The cold hard realization hit her; he wasn't going to ever put her before his job. Empty promises were not going to fix this but she knew that if she kept dragging out this fight he would only retreat more into his work. But she had to try one more time. "You're still going? What about everything you just said? Were you just telling me what you thought I needed to hear? I know you don't want to hear it anymore."

John ignored her and moved over to the bed to zip up his suitcase, grabbing the handle along with his other belongings; he walked back over to Sam, kissed her on her forehead and headed for the door. "I have to, believe me I don't want to go, not now, but I have to. I can't cancel. I'll call you when I land. Love you!"

Samantha stood frozen in the middle of her bedroom, feeling more alone than ever, rehashing the argument they had just had, not sure what to think or feel. "You can take your fresh start and shove it up your ass!" Samantha strolled over towards the bedroom window and watched as the town car pulled away from the house. *Ok, John, since you want me to find my own happiness, I will. And I know exactly where to look. Since you are too busy for me, I know someone who isn't. And he will be more than happy to comply. Now all I need to do is find my damn phone and a sexy outfit. Mr. Miller, you have no idea how lucky you're about to get...*

CHAPTER TWENTY-SIX

It was a good thing Elizabeth was out of town visiting her sister Lori. This left her husband open and available. He was only too willing to come over and 'comfort' Samantha. She made sure she was ready for his arrival. Not wanting to engage in any long conversation, she dressed with minimal clothing sure to entice her lover. When she heard the front door open, she would be ready for him.

Samantha heard Derek's footstep as he climbed the stairs and stalked down the hall. He knocked lightly on her bedroom door and pushed it open. He looked tired, worn, maybe even a bit nervous, but by god he looked hot as hell in his khaki shorts and white t-shirt. His biceps bulged out of the cotton material; his hair was still damp from his morning shower.

He walked over to the bed and sat next to her on the edge. She could see the desire in his eyes and felt the heat radiate off his skin. "Hi.' He spoke softly as he reached up and tucked a lock of her silky brown hair behind her ear.

"Sam, I'm so glad you returned my call; it has been I don't know how long, too long and I really need." Samantha raised her finger and gently placed it on his soft lips to silence him. She had agreed to see him even though she wasn't sure she was ready to hear what he had to say. The minute he had appeared in her doorway, she had felt the electricity flow between them. She couldn't explain why or how, but as soon as he was near she wanted to feel his touch. For her own selfish needs, she needed to feel his warmth; she was drawn to him like a bee to honey. This was her moment to close another chapter in her life, but not without one final love making.

Samantha stared into his amazing blue eyes that were filled with want; she bit her bottom lip, debating the right way to handle this. *Don't do it Sam, you're asking for trouble, he already showed the signs, oh what's one little kiss? What's the harm, right? I need this, I'm tired of feeling alone, deal with it later.* She leaned in and kissed him. His lips were so full and luscious. Derek immediately responded. He wrapped his arms around her waist, pulling her up on his lap. His pressed his soft lips back firmly against hers. Her mouth opened to his and their tongues worked in circles. *He's such a god damn good kisser.* Samantha was losing all sense of control with one kiss. His erection grew bigger against her pelvis, she couldn't fight it, and their chemistry was undeniable.

Everything inside her head screamed, don't do it, but her body wouldn't let her stop. She ached for him; her body screamed to be touched. Samantha pulled back from the heated kiss and slid down his lap onto the floor at his knees. She unbuttoned his shorts and Derek leaned back on the palm of his hands to lift off the bed while she pulled them down around his ankles.

She took all of him in her mouth, sliding up and down in one smooth motion. "Fuck yeah" Derek moaned as her tongue swirled around the top of his arousal. "Oh Sam, you know just how I like it."

Grabbing a fistful of hair he tilted her head back to look into her big emerald green eyes. Samantha knew he loved watching her down on her knees. He was fully erect and still growing with each aching moment.

"Don't make me come yet, baby; you keep that up and it won't be much longer. God, have I missed you; you're so god-damn fucking hot."

Derek pulled Samantha by the arm to stand up. He used his thumb to wipe away the saliva glistening on her lower lip. He stepped out of his shorts and flip flops, guiding her back on the bed, then he pulled his t-shirt off. Samantha lay sprawled on the bed while Derek caressed her with both hands. "Your skin is so soft and smooth." Derek caressed her body, each fingertip lightly sending shockwaves through her veins.

His kisses slowly trailed from her ankle, to the top of her inner thighs spreading her legs further apart. He pushed up her sundress and hooked one finger on the side of her satin thong, moving it over while he lowered his mouth between her legs. Using his finger to spread her further, he licked her again, and her entire body spasmed.

Derek always knew how to make Samantha's toes curl; she felt the tingling sensation begin to grow low within her gut. She rocked back and forth into Derek, grabbing the top of his head, wrapping her legs around his shoulders. He knew just how to bring her to the edge of her orgasm and slow down before her body gave in to the sweet release. She called out his name over and over begging for him to bring her to climax. He traced his kisses over her stomach and kissed each breast as he pulled the rest of her dress over her head. Derek already had a little square foil wrapper in hand; she hadn't seen him grab for it or even where it had come from, but she didn't care. "Derek, hurry up, I need you now!" Derek tilted his head back and laughed out loud while rolling back the rubber on his engorged length. He leaned into her, pushing aside her thong again and with one hard thrust he was inside her, a low growl escaping from his throat. They moved into one another hard and fast, all the built up energy of not being together for weeks was being unleashed. He pushed back the hair from her face. God, she was beautiful and he had her, she was his, he couldn't think straight without her. He cupped her cheeks in both hands and leaned downed to kiss her. Sweat beaded down from the side of his forehead. His hard stomach muscles rippled with each movement. "I love being with you Sam, it feels too good, like it was meant to be."

Samantha's body tensed, she knew there was something more he wanted to say. She knew it had been a mistake to call him and now she just wanted it to be done. She leaned back further into the pillow, closing her eyes as she let out a low satisfied moan, her legs beginning to shake around his body. He grabbed her hips and gave one last hard pump to bring himself to climax with her, then collapsed onto the bed next to her. Wrapping his arms around her, he planted sweet kisses on the top of her head.

Afterwards Samantha was satisfied; she no longer needed Derek there. All she wanted was to drift off and take a nap. He was a means to an end. That was all. Trying to think of a way to escape Derek's needy eyes, she lay facing away from him. Samantha knew that if she said one word he would say something stupid, something that he wouldn't be able to take back. How could she tell him that today all she needed was a good lay, an emotional escape from her fight with John and her sudden relapse into depression? She didn't want to hurt him but she wanted him gone. Just as she was about to ask him to leave, Derek opened his mouth and she knew that this was it.

"That was fucking amazing," Derek breathed. He grinned, displaying that sweet dimple she found so adorable. Samantha was spooned into his arms while Derek rubbed his hands up and down her back in slow motion. "Sam, I'm glad you finally returned my call, I've missed you. Listen, I've been trying to-" his words trailed off. Samantha rolled over and raised her head to look at him while he spoke. She was about to interrupt him, saying anything just so she didn't have to hear the next thing out of his mouth. But it was too late.

"I love you, Samantha."

CHAPTER TWENTY-SEVEN

"You what?" Samantha knew that was what he had intended to tell her but she lay there frozen as if giving him a way out. Take it back, she thought. Can't you see this is not what I want to hear; look at me, and say it was a mistake, anything? Just take it back! I should know better than letting it get this far, I know the warning signs by now, I even picked up on them, my own selfish needs keep getting me in this predicament. He was lying there as if he had just torn out his heart and handed it to her on a golden platter. He had no reason to believe that he just made the biggest mistake. "Oh, Derek." Samantha slowly rose out of bed and was fishing for her sundress.

Derek leaned up on one elbow watching her; he couldn't take his eyes away. "Baby, I mean it. I love you, and I want to be the one that..."

Samantha whipped around and held her hand up for him to stop. "Just stop right there, Derek! This is not how it's supposed to work; this is just sex, that's it. I thought we both understood that." She was hoping he would realize what a mistake he had made and would come to his senses. Instead he just looked at her with love in his eyes. She couldn't take it anymore, she wanted him out of her bed and gone. She found her sundress and started to dress; he was still lying there not moving. "You are making no sense, Derek. You can't love me."

He continued to watch her struggle with the straps of her dress in amusement. He knew she was becoming anxious. He loved her and was willing to do whatever it took for her to see how much. He swung his legs over the side of the bed, leaning down to retrieve his shorts and boxers while disposing of the condom and wrapper in a tissue from the bedside table. Samantha had finished dressing and was running her fingers through her long hair to untangle any knots. Once Derek had his shorts on, he walked over to Samantha and reached for her arm, with his t-shirt in his hand. "I do love you, Sam. And I know you love me, I can feel it. Don't fight it, we can make it work."

"You are crazy. I told you from the very beginning after our first kiss that I had no intention of leaving my husband, you agreed! We agreed! We both knew what this was, a distraction from our everyday lives, some fun. Now you want to be with me?" Samantha gritted her teeth, pulling away from his grip. She needed him to understand that he was acting on impulse, out of lust, not love.

"Sam, I am crazy…I'm crazy about you. You're beautiful; when I'm around you, all I want is to touch you. I love you, can't you see that?" Panic set in, he just needed her to listen and hear him out. He ran his hand through his hair frantically. "Just listen to me, please. I know what you need, want, desire. John doesn't know what he's got. I want to show you how a man's supposed to be. He doesn't give you the attention you deserve. He's never here for you and I know that's what you want. It's what you need. You can't tell me after all these months that you don't have feelings for me? I know you feel it. I see how you look at me. John will never give you what you deserve; he will never be the man you need. Never."

"SHUT UP!" She knew part of what he was saying was true, but he had no right to question her relationship, her marriage. This was her doing though, and she only had herself to blame, but to stand there and act as if he knew about her marriage was more then she could take. He wasn't calling the shots, she was. "How dare you stand there and criticize my marriage! What do you know about it? You're the fucking neighbor that I screw on occasion. Now you think you have a license to tell me about my marriage? My husband? I think you have it wrong, Derek. So wrong."

"Oh come on, he's never here for you, I'm the one you wrap your legs around even when he IS in town. I'm the one you turn to when you need someone not him. When was the last time he held you? How many times do you beg him to stay home with you and he doesn't listen. Sure, he tells you he loves you but he's only pacifying you, Sam. He knows exactly what to say so that you'll leave him alone.

"Let me ask you this, does he even want children? I'm beginning to think John only loves himself and his cell phone. Surely you notice he never puts it down, ever. I wouldn't do that to you. You would have all my attention. You wouldn't have to beg for me to hold you or to stay with you." She stood there seething, Derek didn't seem to notice or care; he wasn't done.

"I know you want babies. Let me give you all the babies you desire, we can do it together, Sam. We'll make a great team and our children will have so much love. We can give them everything they need. Please, Sam, think of it, our babies. Our family."

Samantha couldn't believe he had taken it this far but he seemed desperate. She couldn't stand it anymore, the way he looked at her with pleading eyes, waiting for her to run into his arms and proclaim her love.

"You son of a bitch! How dare you! How fucking dare you! You have no right! You think you can stand here and make accusations about my husband? You think by telling me you can give me babies that I will run off with you? You are fucking delusional! All in one breath you rip my marriage, my husband and me apart and then you claim that you love me? HA! What a fucking joke, Derek. You barely know me. Go home to your wife and baby!" She gritted her teeth as she fought to fight the tears she felt building. Tears of anger or loss were starting to build but she was not about to let this man see her cry. All she wanted was for him to leave.

Derek looked baffled; she was sure this was not how he had played this scene in his head, and this was not how it was supposed to go. It was too late for him to take some of his words back. She didn't care if he had never meant to hurt her, or he just wanted to show her how much he loved her. Maybe attacking her marriage was not his intention, but Derek knew her marriage was in trouble; otherwise she wouldn't be here with him. Hell, his marriage was in just as much trouble.

Derek reached for her again, trying to hide his shaking hands; she pushed away. She didn't care if she hurt him.

"Sam, I know I'm not mistaken, I know you love me too. What about my picture, I know you took my picture." He grinned as if he had uncovered the big mystery.

Samantha avoided his eyes and turned her gaze from his. She knew that he had seen it that day. He must have been waiting for the right moment to bring the picture up. Damn it. How could he possibly think that one picture missing from his home was a testament of love? She looked right at him then. "I don't know what you're talking about."

"Don't lie to me, Sam. You know exactly what I am talking about. That first day I came over with Starbucks and came up here, you were so nervous. I thought it was because we were about to make love for the first time, but it wasn't, was it? You were scurrying around trying to hide that you had taken the picture of me. Those colors. I'd recognize them anywhere. I saw it there on the floor crumpled up. I wouldn't miss that Tampa Bay Rays blue anywhere. If it wasn't for Lizzie asking about its disappearance I may not have put two and two together. So there you go, Sam, you took the picture to have, to look at when you were lonely. It only proves that you love me. You need me."

Stupid bitch notices everything. My God, these two are pathetic. She laughed out loud. "Look I don't know what you're referring to or what you think you saw, but I don't have any pictures of you. You and Elizabeth need some professional help if you think that I stole a picture from your house.

"Seriously, Derek, if I wanted a picture of you I could take one with my phone at any time. This is so laughable, I can't even discuss it anymore. But what I can discuss is you leaving. It's time, time for you to leave for good. This conversation is over. Here me loud and clear for I am only going to say this once. I don't love you. Never have and never will. You can offer me all the babies you want and I will still never love you! And I'm certainly not leaving my husband for you! All you were to me was a great lay, Derek, THAT'S IT! IT'S DONE!"

Samantha stormed out of the bedroom with Derek in tow. She wanted him gone. He had made her feel so pathetic, his words had cut to her core. She felt her stomach twisting and the bile inside rise to her throat; was she going vomit? Had she ever been upset enough to actually throw up?

"I'm not through." Derek followed her downstairs into the living room. He grabbed her shoulders and leaned in; his face was so close to hers she could feel his sweet breath. "I love you, please…don't walk away." He cupped her face and kissed her tenderly. Tears began to stream down her cheeks. She couldn't fight them anymore. She melted into his embrace before realizing what she was giving into. "I know what you've been through. I know the miscarriages have been devastating; please let me be the one to wipe away the pain. Please let me be the one to give you your babies. Please."

Right then something snapped within her. He had crossed a line. "You really have some nerve mentioning my miscarriages as a weapon to get into my pants. I opened up to you, I trusted you. You know the first time you mentioned babies I let it go but now I see, I see how you are using my misfortunes as a way for your sick mind to coerce me into bed. Sorry, asshole, not going to work. If anything, you sicken me. You are the lowest form of a man that there is; you can say all you want about my husband but he would never stoop so low. You need to leave." She pushed him away towards the front door, wiping her eyes. The last thing she wanted was for him to see her upset, but he caught a tear sliding down her cheek.

"Oh, Sam, baby, I'm sorry, I would never use your tragedy to get you into bed. I thought you knew me better than that. How cold do you think I am? How could you think I would do such a thing? I love you! I don't want to make you cry. Please, let me comfort you. Please, you have to believe me!"

Opening the door she guided him out onto the front porch. "It's too late, the damage is done. I don't want you! You are no longer welcome here! Go home to Lizzie and the baby, they need you now more than I ever could!" With that she slammed the door and locked it. Samantha didn't even wait to make sure he was gone, she ran up the stairs into the bathroom and threw up.

Derek heard the dead bolt click into place. He banged a few times yelling for her to open up, but he knew she wasn't letting him back in. He leaned his forehead against the door and sulked for a moment. "What the fuck just happened, where did I go wrong? This was not supposed to happen like this."

Derek pulled himself together and turned around to walk home. Walking off Samantha's front porch he heard a woman humming. It grew louder, almost as if she was calling to him. He wanted to keep walking but there was a force almost carrying him to where the sound was coming from. He looked up and out towards the street; no one was there. He strolled over to the side of the porch and looked around the side bush. The humming was turning into a sing-song, growing louder as he approached the other side of the shrub that separated the Bennett's home from their neighbors. As he turned the corner, there stood Mrs. Kowalski in her denim overalls rolled at the ankles, with her plaid button down shirt and big straw sun hat. She was resting one arm on her broom looking in his direction. "The last thing I need is to bother with this old bat now," he groaned to himself while cupping the back of his neck. "Did you say something, Mrs. Kowalski? Is everything ok?"

She continued singing, looking right at him but was barely making any sense. At first he couldn't understand what she was saying but the longer he stood there looking at her asking her if she needed anything, the louder her voice became and he finally understood what she was chanting. "When the cat's away the mice will play."

"I'm sorry, what?"

"When the cat's away, the mice will play. You are not the first and you won't be the last."

"The first, last what? Mrs. Kowalski, what are you trying to say?"

"Oh, Mr. Miller, you know exactly what I'm saying. You are just another pawn in her game; her game of lies and deception. Her poor husband….Tsk Tsk…What he doesn't know will hurt him." She then pointed to Derek and looked him dead in the eye, shaking her finger at him. "You are not special to her. No one is." She laughed. He was about to interrupt her when she continued, "You're just like the other fellow who lived here before you. Ruined his family. Ran away like thieves. You should run too, Mr. Miller. Run, run away fast before she destroys you and your pretty little family."

"Mrs. Kowalski, I don't know what you are talking about, I really don't. Please, can I help you back into your house?"

She laughed again and then stopped. With serious eyes she walked right up to Derek. "That woman is pure evil. Run, Mr. Miller. Don't look back. Save your family before it's too late." She turned back around and headed over to her front stoop.

He stood there with his mouth open in disbelief. He was utterly confused. He wanted to go after the old lady, ask her more questions but instead he started back to his house. His conversation with Samantha was still fresh on his mind but what Mrs. Kowalski had said was burning in his brain. Her words started to take form, like pieces of a puzzle fitting together. Mrs. Kowalski might not be delusional after all. She might just be the one to save his marriage.

CHAPTER TWENTY-EIGHT

You are not the first and you won't be the last, you're just like the other fellow who lived here before you. Derek couldn't get the words out of his head. He barely made it through the front door without tripping over himself. He couldn't believe that everything that had transpired between him and Sam was a lie. It just didn't make sense. Was he a pawn in her game? Had he fallen right into her trap? Was he so delusional that he'd let her manipulate him? He couldn't think straight, every word spoken between Samantha and him was running through his mind. She loved him, without a doubt she was crazy about him as much as he was about her. Yes, there were major obstacles in the way but in the end they would make it work. Why couldn't she see it, admit it to herself? He needed to find out if this was all a game to her. He needed to have answers. "Well, if Sam isn't going to give them to me than I know where to look."

Derek tried to focus on the task at hand; find the Patterson's address. Not sure of what his exact move would be, he just knew he needed to find it. Derek scrambled through the kitchen pulling out drawers and opening cabinets, dropping all the items out of them; papers, pens, and a mini calendar went flying. He dropped a stapler on his foot and yelped in pain. He was frantic; he couldn't let the pain throbbing in his foot stop him from searching. His chest was tight, restricting him from taking full deep breaths. "I know I saw it, where the fuck did I put it? God, I hope Lizzie didn't throw it away."

The telephone began to ring, but Derek ignored it; he didn't have time to answer any calls. He knew it wouldn't be Samantha. After the fifth ring the answering machine clicked in. "Hi Derek, it's me. Just wanted to call and check in. I guess you're out. If you want call me on my cell when you get this." Elizabeth's voice was soft and uneasy, but Derek still didn't stop moving. He was shaking with rage, stepping over a drawer on the floor that had fallen off the track; he bent down and threw papers to the side. Just as he was about to give up in the kitchen and move on to his office he caught sight of an envelope with 'return to sender' written across the front. AHA! BINGO! Mr. Pete Patterson. Derek sighed with relief. His nerves relaxed, allowing him to take in a deep breath. He wasn't really planning on doing anything with it, but it was as if someone else had taken over his body and before he knew it he was in his office pulling up Google maps.

Derek typed the forwarding address on the envelope into the search bar and within seconds the man's address with directions were staring him in the face. He sat there for a minute and debated. He knew this was crazy but he also knew that he wouldn't rest until he had all the answers. He looked to see if there was a phone number listed but it was private. Damn! This leaves me no choice. Again, Mrs. Kowalski's warning ran through his mind. *You are not the first and you won't be the last, you're just like the other fellow who lived here before you.* If he was going to do this he needed to do it now. He printed the directions and left the house, grabbing his car keys on the way out.

Having a good two hour drive ahead allowed his mind to wander. Samantha's harsh words had cut right through him. He had never meant to hurt her. Never in a million years was he trying to use her miscarriages as a way to seduce her. How could she think that? What the fuck was going on? Was she just using him? He had confessed his love for her and she had ripped his heart in two, stomping on it as she kicked him out. They both had said things out of anger, but one thing he knew for sure was that he loved her. Didn't he?

He tried to find a radio station to take his mind off their conversation but he couldn't find anything to dull the pain he was feeling. He was trying to sort through all his emotions. He felt sad, then angry, and then confused and desperate. He was dizzy with the old bat's words swirling around in his head like a merry go round on speed. Shit, maybe we all underestimated the old bag; perhaps there is truth to her crazy rants! *Run, run away fast before she destroys you and your pretty little family.* He didn't know what was true or false at this point; he slammed his hand on the steering wheel out of frustration, while Mrs. Kowalski's words haunted him. Luckily he made it over the bridge without hitting any major traffic, which was a godsend considering there was always bumper to bumper traffic; the last thing he needed was more aggravation. He merged onto the I – 95 north and continued to drive with a little more ease.

Realizing he was getting closer to his destination, he tried to think of what to do, what to say. He had no plan. He had no real proof that this man had had an affair with Samantha. But something in him knew that he had. *This really is insane; maybe she's right, maybe I am crazy? Have I lost my ever loving mind? What normal man drives off to some stranger's house to do what? Ask for proof that he was sleeping with his lover? To pick a fight with a man he knew nothing about?* Too late, he wanted answers and he wasn't going to leave the man's house until he got them.

When he reached his exit, he tightened his hands around the steering wheel, his knuckles turning white. He felt like a fucking fool. Again he started to have doubts as to what he was doing. Seriously, what was he going to do? Kick the shit out of the guy? Why was he so pissed off at this man? He was the one who was about to show up on his doorstep. This guy was probably a fool just like him, believing her lies and allowing her to seduce him with her captivating green eyes, luscious lips and long legs, god he loved it when they were wrapped around him. *Stop man! Think straight.* He couldn't control his thoughts. He followed the last directions from his GPS, and turned onto the street.

There it was, the house on Oxford Drive that held the answers. It was a Cape-style home on what looked to be about a half an acre property, detached garage, nice quiet street. Derek parked across the street and watched the house for a bit, trying to collect his thoughts. He began to feel a bit queasy. This wasn't him; he didn't make surprise visits to random people's homes. But then, he had never thought that he would cheat on his wife, he should have had more self-control. What went wrong? Feeling sorry for himself, he stepped out of the car and slowly walked up to the front door observing his surroundings. He didn't want to be here anymore, but he had to know the truth.

Rehearsing what he was going to say, he hesitantly knocked on the front door. He stood with his hands in his front pockets looking nervously around. Any thoughts of what he was preparing to say escaped him as he heard footsteps approaching the front door. He almost turned around and left just as the door opened. The man standing there was older than Derek had expected. He took a deep breath and collected his thoughts.

"Can I help you with something?"

"Uh, yes are you Mr. Pete Patterson?" Derek asked nervously.

"Yes, can I help you?" Derek was confused. *There must be something wrong; I had to have heard Mrs. Kowalski wrong. This man certainly could not have had an affair with Samantha, she couldn't, she wouldn't…*Peter Patterson was maybe about twenty to thirty years older than Sam. He had salt and pepper hair, deep gray eyes set far apart, a sharp chin, round nose, a little heavy around the sides; he may have been an attractive man once in his day, but Derek couldn't see Sam having an affair with this guy. *Maybe I went to his father's home?*

"Son, is there something you need? I am a busy man. If you're here to sell me something, don't bother. I don't need internet service, I am very happy with my telephone provider and my burial plot is already picked out and paid for. So if there isn't anything else, I'll have to say goodbye."

"I – uh, I'm sorry, I'm Derek Miller. I'm not here to sell you anything sir. I'm sorry. You know I shouldn't be here. I should just go. This was a mistake." Derek had started to turn and walk away when the man stopped him.

"Son, you look like the weight of the world is on your shoulder. What is that you need? Car break down? Need a tow? What's your name? David?"

"Derek. Derek Miller. And no my car didn't break down. And you're right; I do need something from you. I just can't believe I'm here." He shook his head in disbelief.

"Well, Derek. You're here so spill it. I can see your plates are from New York, so you drove here to Connecticut for something. Do I know you? What do you need from me? I don't have all day, so let's get to the point."

"No sir you don't know me. I guess I should start at the beginning. I bought your old house on Long Island, New York and this was left behind." Derek pulled out the folded envelope with the bill inside. The man's face shifted from confusion to worry. He opened the screen door pulling the storm door shut behind him as he stepped down onto the front stoop.

"You came all this way just to bring by an old bill?" Peter's brow furrowed. "Ok, what do you want, and don't lie to me.

228

You could have mailed this to me. What do you want?" He glared at Derek.

Derek shifted back and forth on his feet; he kicked at a pebble on the walkway. Peter waited impatiently for him to answer. "Samantha Bennett," Derek said quietly.

Peter's face drained of all color. Derek didn't know what to make of it, but it wasn't good. Peter kept looking over his shoulder as if to see if anyone was in ears reach. "I think it's best that you leave. We don't speak of that woman's name here."

Derek stood frozen. He wasn't about to leave, now that he actually brought it up, it was very obvious to him that he had the right man. "Sir, please. I need to know. My life has been turned upside down. I don't know what to do. Please."

Peter grabbed Derek by the arm and began to drag him down the walkway towards his car. Again he kept looking over his shoulder. "Listen to me and listen to me good, you get in your car and drive away now. I don't know why you came out here to confront me about a woman who... never mind, just go."

"So you did. You had an affair with her? Please. I need to know what happened. Mrs. Kowalski said..."

"That old bat should be ready for a pine box by now, but one thing she knows is that woman and her evil ways. She always meddles in other people's business though. She warned me. But I didn't listen. Old fucking fool I was. Thinking of my needs only....Just leave!" The man loosened his grip on Derek's arm,

"Wait, can't you just answer my question? Did you have an affair with her? Were there others? I need to know."

229

The older man laughed. He faced Derek head on and looked him straight in the eye. "You don't need to know shit. What you need is to get away from her. It's a chapter of my life that is buried. She nearly destroyed my family. Listen up, buddy, you aren't the first and neither was I. From the looks of it you have a wife and maybe a kid or two? I suggest you go home and beg for their forgiveness, if it isn't too late."

"I do, a son, he's a baby. And a wife that I adore. I don't know what I was thinking..."

"You weren't. You were thinking with your dick. Let me guess, she piled it on right? Lonely, can't have kids, husband is gone all the time? Yeah, yeah. Good old Samantha. She used you boy, used you and then tossed you aside. That's what she does."

He stood there practically laughing at Derek. *Serves me right,* Derek thought.

"Why?"

The older man looked at him. "Because you let her." And with that he turned and walked up the driveway, leaving Derek standing there in his grief.

CHAPTER TWENTY-NINE

Packing her Coach overnight bag, Samantha felt jittery. Relief had set in when Lauren had texted her to see if she wanted to have a girls' weekend at her apartment. Wine, cheese and crackers, a couple of girlfriends and lots of chick flicks were just what she needed in order to keep her mind off of Derek. What would be Derek's next move? Would he tell his wife? Would he tell John?

Vomit started rising in her throat. "Not again."

Samantha jolted up off the floor where she was packing her bag and made a beeline for the bathroom, covering her mouth. She rested one arm over the toilet bowl while the other pinned her hair back away from her face. Her stomach clenched and she bucked forward, face in the bowl.

After emptying everything she had and then some, she leaned back, wiping her mouth with a towel. "Sam, you really need to calm down, your nerves are getting the best of you. Nothing is going to happen. If Derek was going to spill the beans, he would have already right? Sam, you better come up with damage control just in case. First you need to stop talking to yourself and get some Pepto-Bismol." Samantha sat on the bathroom floor for a bit longer as her stomach started to settle, then she stood up, grabbing her robe off the back of the bathroom door, and headed into the kitchen.

After finding the pink stuff she gulped some down and chugged some water. She was standing in front of the window above the sink. The same window that she first saw Derek through. Seemed like a lifetime time ago, but in reality it was just months. She wanted to peek through the curtain to see what was going on at Derek's house. She was just about to take a peek but stopped herself. Stupid, she thought, I can't care anymore.

There was a part of her that regretted sending Derek away, she liked him. He was different from all the others. She reached for her cell. What am I doing? I can't text him. Not now. She put her phone down then and went to return to her packing but something was nagging at her. Just one quick peek, it won't hurt. And she did.

She slowly moved the bottom right hand corner of the curtain and peeked through. Nothing. No cars were in the driveway, nothing. Hmmm. I guess they went out. That's a good sign; if he told his wife I'm sure they would be home fighting. What woman would go to work if she just found out her husband was cheating on her? Not Elizabeth, that's for sure. Mrs. Perfect would never want to admit that her perfect husband was a cheat. She shrugged and went back up to her room to pack.

Still she felt uneasy. *Getting away from here for a couple of days is just the distraction I need. John isn't due home for a few more days so that gives me plenty of time to get my shit together and get back to normalcy around here.* Samantha looked at the clock. *The girls will be expecting me soon.*

Stuffing the last of her belongings inside her bag, something came over Samantha. She couldn't shake the feeling. A feeling she hadn't felt in a long time. She stood there frozen. She felt so alone, lost. She felt defeated and deflated, like a balloon that had lost its air. Willing herself to move, she started to walk. One foot in front of the other, she kept telling herself. And when she stopped she wasn't at the bedroom door leaving; instead she found herself in her closet.

She looked around at her belongings. Her blouses hung neatly, color coordinated, hung by sleeve length. Her jeans were folded perfectly in their custom-made drawers divided by boot cut, skinny or wide legged. Scarfs hung divided by color and length. Her designer handbags were placed like trophies on shelves, organized by season and designer. Perfect. Everything in this closet, her closet, was perfectly organized and laid out. If a stranger walked in, they would think a woman who had it all lived there. This woman had a life that many women dreamed of. Everything in its place. So perfect. So put together. Picture perfect. If only that was the truth.

Samantha didn't know why or what pushed her to do what she did next but she reached up on her top shelf and pulled down her wedding shoebox. She felt around underneath the tissue paper and pulled out a key. This one little key was the most important item in Samantha's world. It was the answer to all of her pain, all of her deepest and darkest secrets and all of who Samantha was.

She reached up in the back of her closet and brought down the locked box. Putting the key in the hole with shaky hands, Samantha took a deep breath in. Once the cover was lifted and she had scanned the contents inside, she let a long breath out.

These were her memories, items that she could look back on and remember what it felt like to be happy, wanted, and almost complete at times. She sat down on the floor and ran her fingers over the contents in the box. A surge of emotions went through her. She didn't want to cry, she wanted to remember. She wanted to go back to the places and times that all these mementoes held. Here alone in her picture perfect closet with her mementoes, no one could tell her to make a fresh start; no one could tell her who she was or was supposed to be. Here with her box of sentiments she felt alive. She felt in control.

On top of the pile of trinkets was her family photo. She picked it up and traced her fingers across her mother's face. She remembered standing there in between her mother and father; her father was a tall handsome man smiling proudly with his arm around his wife and the other hand resting on Samantha's shoulder. Her mother, Jane, had a heart of gold and a beautiful face to match. Samantha was the spitting image of her sweet mother on the outside, the big emerald green eyes, silky brown hair, but when it came to Samantha and her ways, the apple didn't fall too far from the tree...her father's tree that is.

When her father left, it destroyed them. She would never forgive him for ruining their happy home. A part of her blamed him for the way she had turned out. Wanting it all, never having enough, nothing making her happy or feeling complete. How different would she be if he had stayed?

Underneath the family photo was the sonogram pictures of Alexa Jane; she nearly choked on her sobs when she lifted it up to her chest. Samantha would never forget what pain she had endured losing her. All her hopes and dreams came crashing in on her when she was told about her baby girl. The baby she would never hold. The baby she would never see grow up. All her life Samantha had wanted to be a mommy. She wanted to bake cookies, fix boo-boo's, go to PTA meetings. She had dreamt about being a mommy ever since she could remember. Why was her baby taken from her? What did she do that was so bad that she didn't deserve a baby? It wasn't fair. It was cruel. And she had hated the world for the longest time.

Sure, John had tried to be supportive but he would never understand what it was like to lose a part of you. In some small way she blamed John. Shit, she blamed everyone. When she ran out of people to blame she had no choice but to look at herself. She was to blame. Maybe if she had been a better person. Maybe if she had been skinnier or prettier or more supportive of her husband, maybe then she could have her baby. But she was all those things. She was damn near perfect in the looks department, had a figure to kill for and a face that could be in magazines, or so she had been told on many occasions. And she supported her husband one hundred percent and never complained about the constant texting, or phone calls or last minute trips.

And still no baby. Instead she was told to move on and make a fresh start. No matter how many times she tried, she couldn't replace her baby. And now all she was left with was a picture of what should have been. A constant reminder of what she had lost. Mourning for her baby girl.

As she placed her baby's sonogram picture down, she wished that one day she and John would have a child to love and cherish. She wasn't sure if they ever would now.

She wiped away her tears, and chuckled to herself when she looked down and saw the plastic pin that surprisingly still blinked 'Zorbas'. It was a pin from an old restaurant where she and Lauren used to have lunch, but once things became a bit complicated with Demetrius, Samantha's first affair, she had to find a better, more appealing Greek restaurant for meeting up with her friend. Demetrius, had been young, in his second year in college, working as a bus boy to help pay for tuition, but he was super sweet, a lot of fun and loved nothing more than to please Samantha. All she had to do was smile and bat her eyes at him and he was putty. Things went well for a while; she would meet him at hotels just outside of town, or they would fool around in a movie theater, but he fell in love and became obsessed. Samantha had to put the kibosh on that. It was hard at first, but he eventually gave up.

Next came Billy; she lifted up his business card and read it out loud. William Shaw *Assistant Director of Financial Operations.* Samantha had enjoyed working with Billy. It was tricky at times, especially in the accounting office they worked in, but they made it happen. This affair ended when he was promoted and had to relocate, but she knew he wouldn't have lasted much longer, he was sending all the signals for Samantha to end their relationship. After Billy, Samantha had tried to gain control of her life and wicked ways, but after months and months of trying to conceive a child with her husband, and it just wasn't happening, she was lost again and John was working more and more it seemed.

That's when good ole Pete stepped in. He was much older than Samantha but she didn't mind. As crazy and twisted as it may sound, he reminded her of her father or how she imagined he would have been. Pete adored Samantha, and he was full of charisma. Samantha was looking for comfort and Pete was the man for the job.

She picked up his watch out of her locked box. She had stolen it from him the very first time they had had sex. It was just there for the taking; she hadn't realized she had it until she was home after leaving his bed.

The affair with Pete lasted a while. One of her longest, their relationship was working out perfectly; he worked the grave-yard shift at one of the local trucking companies as a dispatcher and his wife worked as a clerk in the town hall. That left a lot of alone time during the afternoon for the two of them, since she worked mornings. But as time went on, Pete began to freak Samantha out. He became too clingy, always wanting to know who she was with and where she was or what she was doing. At times, he became angry with her if she couldn't see him for a day. That break up was not easy, and to be honest she became afraid of him. Before the Patterson's vanished, Samantha became pregnant for the first time.

Throwing Pete's watch back into the box, she saw the crinkled photo of Derek. There he was standing in his Tampa Bay Rays jersey accepting his award. Oh sweet sexy Derek. Her heart began to pound and the tears started to pool at her lids. He was the reason she was feeling this horrible at the moment.

Crazy that at one point she had pictured what her life would have been if it was Derek she had married instead of John. She enjoyed their conversations. She actually felt comfortable around him and was able to share things with him that she couldn't with John.

"Oh, Derek, I'll miss you." Again she started to panic. Would he tell Elizabeth? Why would he? He wouldn't; he had more to lose out of this than she did. He wouldn't take the chance of losing his son, would he? He wouldn't be so stupid, or careless. *I need to stop this worrying. I'm going to end up in a crazy house. Deep breath girl. Nothing is going to happen.* As if on cue her stomach started to do flips, cramps were coming on strong. Samantha ran for the bathroom, only this time she wasn't going to throw up, she was going to be glued to the bowl.

After her last episode in the bathroom Samantha hopped into the shower, changed clothes, pushed her lock box into the back of her closet and left for Lauren's.

This time she had no choice but to look at Derek's house while pulling out of the driveway. Still no cars, she didn't take any chances and went the opposite way down the block. She kept looking in her rearview mirror while driving away but nobody was there. It was quiet, too quiet.

On her way to Lauren's, Samantha had time to think. She pushed her anxiety aside in hopes of keeping her stomach at bay. She let her mind wander to her past digressions.

The one that kept making its way to the front of her conscious was Pete. A little older, but boy did he have charisma. That's what had attracted her to him. He had made her laugh and the way he looked at her made her melt. Not her normal type at all, but there was something so sexy about him.

It was a shame it had ended. It had ended badly; she really feared he would tell John. Rejection was not part of Pete's MO. But he was becoming too clingy, always wanting to know where she was, what she was doing. *I don't have that issue with John,* she would tell him. But Pete didn't care. He wanted her and he wanted her to only want him.

He got creepy, leaving her notes, texting her; something was off with him. When she ended it she thought he was going to lose it completely. She feared what he might have done. But luckily, his entire family just disappeared during the night. *I don't care where he is or what he's doing, as long as he stays there, in the past where he belongs.*

CHAPTER THIRTY

Derek pulled into his driveway just before dark. Driving home was a struggle internally. His thoughts were racing between his conversations with both Mrs. Kowalski and Mr. Patterson. Trying to process all that he had learned in the last twenty four hours led to a pounding headache that he knew was not going to go away anytime soon. He was tired, and starved, but all he could think about was crawling into bed. He was drained, still confused and worst of all, he felt used. All his past regressions were coming full circle. He had no one to blame but himself. *No, I blame Sam too. Why would she do this? Why start something so amazing just to end it?* One thing Mr. Patterson had right was that Derek had allowed himself to fall for Samantha. No one had forced him to sleep with her; he did that all on his own. He had cheated on his wife, made a mess of his relationship, and now he had to fix it. Or at least try.

Here he was sitting there in his driveway staring at his front door. Behind that door was where his wife and child lived. Behind that door was his life. Behind that door were all his lies and regrets that he now had to face. The last thing Derek wanted was to end up like Pete Patterson. Samantha must have done a number on him. The man was an asshole, and his affair with Sam hadn't helped him in the self-esteem department either. He was old beyond his years, as if his relationship with Samantha had aged him. Derek didn't want to end up bitter like Pete. He didn't want to end up alone either.

He did love his wife; he had loved Elizabeth since the first day they met years ago. She completed him in ways no one ever had. The move to New York had disrupted their daily routines and the time spent with one another. It was no excuse, but loneliness could drive a person to do things they normally wouldn't do; it could change a person. Driving home from Connecticut, he had realized that. His thoughts were everywhere, but the one thing he knew was that he had to make it right. No matter what it took. He wanted to be a family again, he wanted to be with his wife; having his son should have made him realize sooner the games Samantha was playing, but he was blinded, obsessed and borderline crazy for her.

Climbing his front stoop, he turned around and looked across the street. He stood staring at the Bennett's house, wondering about his lover. There was a part of him that wanted to go over there and confront her, and the other part wanted to tell her that he still loved her, but he knew it was over. It had to be. Her house was dark except for the outside front porch light. John was still away on business; maybe Samantha was in bed already or out with friends. He shook his head, pushing his thoughts of Samantha aside. Putting his key in the lock, he noticed the door was open. *Shit, did I forget to lock it on my way out earlier?* Stepping inside he heard his son crying and Elizabeth comforting him. His heart skipped a beat, listening to his wife with their newborn son. "Lizzie?" Derek called out as he strolled through the living room into the kitchen. Elizabeth stood feeding DJ as he lay strapped in his car seat resting on the kitchen table. He walked over to the carrier and rubbed his hand on the top of his son's head. His son looked up at him with dreamy eyes, still chugging away, patting his fist at the bottle. "Hey, when did you get home?" He looked over at Elizabeth with remorse in his eyes. He scanned the rest of the kitchen and the mess he'd left. It seemed like a lifetime ago that he was in here, trashing the kitchen looking for the envelope. He immediately felt sick; he knew she was pissed and confused. She had every right to be.

Elizabeth didn't seem to notice that Derek was in the kitchen. Her silence was torture. Maybe she was distracted with feeding the baby. But something told him that was not the case. She looked as if she hadn't slept in days. Her hair was pulled back in a loose ponytail, no make-up. She barely looked up at him and continued to feed the baby. He stood there watching her, waiting for her to confront him about the mess he had left. She didn't say a word; she was on auto pilot and was only focused on the baby. He felt like a stranger in his own home, he didn't feel like he belonged there. Elizabeth unbuckled the straps and lifted DJ out of the seat to burp him. The cloth floated off his lap onto the floor; she squatted down to grab it, and pulled the chair out across from Derek as she stood up. He motioned his hands towards the mess. "I know I left a mess, Lizzie, I'm sorry." Complete silence. Elizabeth finished burping the baby on her lap and placed him back in the car seat; he was already asleep once she fastened the last strap. She then walked out of the kitchen into the family room. Her face was turned towards the fireplace mantel where their wedding picture sat. Derek walked behind her; he reached to touch her shoulder, but she turned around and looked at him, really looked at him. And then the words he had feared the most were said, not by him but by her.

"I know, Derek. I know."

She couldn't help but notice that his hair was a mess, his eyes glazed; he looked like a man who had lost a battle before it even began. She almost felt sorry for him, almost. She started to cackle. "Mess? You're sorry you left a mess in the kitchen?" She laughed louder, trying to keep the tears from falling. "What about the fucking mess you made of us? Our marriage? I've known Derek. I've been waiting for you to tell me about your affair with Sam. I was praying and hoping that I was wrong, but that day at the hospital, I knew. All this time while I was at work supporting you, our family, you were …you were screwing the neighbor! What about that mess, Derek? How are you going to clean this up? How? Derek, how? Oh my God, do you love her?" Derek just stood there. "Well, do you?" The tears began to fall.

His heart ached and the daggers she spewed with her words twisted deeply. Reaching for her arms, he stood there, pleading with her through his piercing eyes. "Lizzie, I'm sorry, I'm so sorry, I don't know what to say, or how to make it right." His breathing became heavier; sweat glistened on the top of his brow. "I don't know who I am anymore, ever since moving here. I don't know the man I've become and I don't want to be him. I've been a horrible husband and father." He dropped to his knees in front of her, wrapping his arms around her waist. He began to sob.

"Answer me, Derek. Answer me now. Do you love her?" The words were almost a whisper.

Elizabeth was lifeless, the air had been sucked out of her, she knew it was true, felt it with every bone in her body, even after trying to convince herself it wasn't, but to hear him admit to it…that was a knife through her heart. She waited for him to answer, not sure if she wanted to know. He kept sobbing at her feet, holding on to her. "Do you, Derek? ANSWER ME!" She wanted to keep control of the situation; she refused to break down at this moment but the anger was building inside.

Between sobs he answered softly, "I love you, Lizzie. I don't know what I was thinking. I am so sorry. Please believe me." Derek felt a strange sense of déjà vu . Didn't he just have this same conversation with his lover? What was he doing? He was getting his wife and son back. Samantha was a mistake. He was lonely and stupid. Then why was he still thinking about her?

Elizabeth stood there, thoughts racing in her mind. "Did I do something to make you run to her? Have there been others?

Derek, how many others were there? Why? Why did you do this to me? To us? Why her? Why Derek? What did I do wrong? Tell me. TELL ME!" She backed away from him and paced the floor; she didn't know what do to with all her nervous energy.

Derek slowly stood up. He wiped away his tears, feeling like a piece of shit. She didn't deserve this. "You didn't do anything wrong. Lizzie, there weren't any others. I swear. Please tell me what to do to make this right. I know you will never trust me again. I will do anything you want. She meant nothing to me. She was just there. I was lonely. You were gone a lot and I don't know, we had a lot in common. It just happened. Please believe me, there was and never will be anyone but you."

Elizabeth stopped, taking it all in, listening to his pleas. This move had been extremely hard on both of them, the long hours working, being pregnant, not spending enough time together or making the time. He was wrong on so many levels and she was beyond devastated, but part of her couldn't blame him. He must have been lonely. Samantha was beautiful, what guy would refuse that? She had been hormonal and would lash out over the littlest things. She didn't want to be around herself either at times!

She couldn't look at him; tears began to stream down her cheeks again. She stood still with her arms hanging down her sides. No matter how hard things got, she would never disrespect her husband the way he had her. They had a family though now, it wasn't as easy to just walk away. She wanted DJ to grow up with his father, the man she knew Derek was and could be again given the chance. But could she do that? Was she willing to accept his mistake and move forward? Would she hold it against him every chance she got? Could she ever trust him again?

"Affairs don't just happen, Derek. Let's face facts. We both made some mistakes this past year. Maybe the move here was not such a good idea, but to go fuck the neighbor? Derek, how could you? I would never do this to you. Never. And she is my friend, was my friend. What about John? Does he even suspect anything? I bet he doesn't even have a fucking clue; he's gone half the time anyway.

"Were you both laughing at me and John while the two of you were fucking? Were you fucking her in our bed? Oh my God, Derek? Were you? God please tell me you weren't?" Elizabeth felt sick to her stomach.

"NO! I would never do that!" *What's one more lie?* "Lizzie, stop torturing yourself. Please, can't we just move forward? Tell me what to do. Tell me what you want me to do. I will do anything you want. But please, please don't make me leave. Please, I need you and our son. I need us."

"I don't know Derek. I don't know. I need time. You can stay here. You can sleep in the spare room for now."

He moved closer, enveloping his wife in his arms while they both cried. He didn't know where this left them, but she wasn't pushing him away which was a good start. He was hopeful. He knew better then to tell her what he had discovered that afternoon. He would keep it his secret. For some reason he wanted to protect Samantha. Even after all she had done to him, he wanted to keep her safe.

"I want to move back home," Elizabeth's voice was muffled in his shoulder. She looked up at her husband. Derek used his thumb to brush away her tears. "After seeing my family I realized I want to be back home. I need to leave here, but I can't go back to Florida. Jersey is home for me and I want to raise my son, our son, where I grew up. I've already spoken with the hospital, the transfer is in progress and I can start as soon as possible. I have a job, and I'll stay with family until I find somewhere to live. We need to leave now. I want to be packed and gone by this weekend. You will have to rent a truck, I don't care. I just want out of this house NOW."

Derek stood there, amazed at how strong his wife was. How determined she was. He also knew that he had no choice and he wanted a life with his wife and son. He stood and nodded in agreement and allowed her to make her demands. After all, he had it coming.

"It's your choice. I know the man I married and that's the man I want to be a father to my child, but there is a lot of work to be done here." Elizabeth stepped back, wrapping her arms around her stomach. Her words were emotionless and soft, she felt numb.

"You will need to get a job while finishing your book. I can't stand to live with you at this moment. I can't wake up and see your face every morning, all I see is betrayal. Like I said, tonight you can stay in the spare room. The last thing I want is for that bitch across the street to see you leave and have some sick satisfaction that she stole my husband." Elizabeth stopped in order to not fall apart and took a deep breath, pushing the thought of her friend sleeping with her husband out of her head.

"Once we get to Jersey you need to find an apartment near my sister. Maybe if we're separated we can work on trust. I can't take you away from DJ, he needs you. We need marriage counseling. We need to work out these issues. You hurt me, Derek, you tore my heart out. I never in a million years would have expected that from you. I don't know if I will ever be able to trust you again." Tears began to slide down her face as she lectured him. Derek hated himself for being the one who caused the pain she felt. Guilt started to weigh in; he rubbed his face with both hands as he listened to her demands.

"I can't argue anymore, I want to move forward and try to put this behind me. This is your choice under the circumstances I mentioned, me and DJ or Sam....are you willing to work at keeping your family or does Sam mean that much to you?"

For a quick second he wasn't positive of his answer. He wasn't sure of anything. Not anymore. But he wanted to be with his wife and son. "I want you," was all he could say, and at that moment he meant it.

Elizabeth nodded, realizing that something was missing. After all the tears and all the truths out on the table, not once had Derek said that he never loved Samantha. Not once.

CHAPTER THIRTY-ONE

Turning the corner onto Shore Road, Samantha could feel the anticipation brewing within her. She wanted to start her evening with John. She was much calmer after spending time with her girlfriends. It had been just what she'd needed in order to get her life back on track. She also just wanted to get inside the house as quickly as possible.

Forcing herself to stay focused at the task at hand and not look in the directions of the Miller's home, Samantha had her pocketbook in one hand and her keys in the other. She was ready to jump out of the car and make a dash into the house. The last thing she wanted was to see any of the Miller's.

Too bad her plan didn't work.

There she stood, right in front of her car door. Elizabeth.

Damn, she thought, I don't need this now. She wasn't in the mood. She was beginning to feel in control again after putting her argument with Derek behind her. The waves of nausea would still come and go, but she could handle that, talking to Elizabeth right now was something she couldn't. To top it off, Elizabeth didn't look too happy. She didn't look mad or upset, she just looked indifferent.

Here we go. Samantha smiled at the woman standing there like a statue.

"Hey, Lizzie!" Samantha tried to play it cool as she stepped out of the car. She couldn't let Elizabeth see her sweat. And right now she could feel her face flushing. She needed to keep her poker face on now more than ever. You did not sleep with her husband. Deny, deny, deny.

"Hello Samantha, how are you?" Elizabeth stood with her arms crossed at her chest, just staring. Samantha could have sworn she detected sarcasm in Elizabeth's tone. Who knew perfect little Lizzie could have an attitude? Usually so annoyingly and disgustingly perky, this was a new look for the princess. At the moment it was more like ice princess.

"I'm good, Lizzie. What's up?"

"Funny, Derek, my *husband*, left a few hours ago and I can't seem to locate him now. He's not answering his phone. I thought if anyone would know where he was, *you* would."

"Derek? Huh? I'm sorry, Lizzie, I have no idea where *your* husband is. I can barely keep tabs on mine. Besides, I've been gone all weekend. Girl's weekend. No boys allowed." Samantha laughed. She was quickly becoming aggravated with her neighbor. If you want to know, just ask, she wanted to say; instead she slammed the car door and stood face to face with her ex- lover's wife. Who at the moment was glaring at her as if debating her next move.

"Girl weekend, huh? That sounds like fun, it's nice having girlfriends you can just hang around with, be yourself, and trust. Trust is very important with friends."

There's that tone again. Jesus, lady if you knew about the affair you wouldn't be making small talk. We would be reenacting a bad soap opera scene with hair grabbing and name calling. We wouldn't be playing 'Where's Waldo'.

"Yes, I have some really great girlfriends. I'm sure you had a few back home?" Samantha replied, slowly walking towards her front porch. "You know girl chat, bad movies, dancing and drinks. You ever have a girl's weekend, Elizabeth? Or are you all work and no play? Derek says you haven't had a lot of fun since moving in. Our time together chatting, he's mentioned that you really need to get out more. Let your hair down. Take a lesson from me." *Check mate, bitch.*

"Well, you know how it is, Samantha. Being a new mommy… oh, wait, I'm sorry. You don't, do you?"

Samantha froze, then turned around, forcing the biggest grin she could. Determined not to let the ice princess catch her off guard, Samantha knew what she was up to. She was trying to rattle her cage, make her confess.

What Elizabeth didn't realize was that this was not her first rodeo.

"You're right, Lizzie. I don't. Not yet. But with the way things have been lately…You never know." Take that you bitch, Samantha wanted to snap, but she held her tongue.

"Anyway, Lizzie, if that's all you came here for, to find your hubby, you're out of luck. I have no clue. Maybe you should chip his ass and GPS him." Samantha couldn't help but giggle. This was becoming absurd.

"Maybe I should. Then again you probably should too with John never around. Lord knows what he's up to."

This chick is about to go down. She has no clue who or what she's up against. Keeping her composure, not wanting to allow Elizabeth the satisfaction that she was getting to her, Samantha laughed. "Funny, Lizzie, I never felt the need to go searching for my husband. I never had to play Sherlock to find him by interrogating the locals for his whereabouts. He's a pretty good man. I trust him one hundred percent."

"Aren't you the lucky one then?" It became perfectly clear that Elizabeth was not a stupid woman. Naïve, but not stupid. Maybe she was a formidable opponent after all.

"I guess I am. Well, like I said, I was just coming in from a girl's weekend. I'm exhausted. I'm going to go lie down and then get dinner ready for John. I'm planning a romantic evening for us, so if you don't mind." *Get lost already. I am so done with you and your snide comments.*

"Oh, well, I wouldn't want to ruin your evening. Besides, I'm sure Derek will be home soon. We too have plans. Big plans." Elizabeth started to turn and walk away when she turned around, "Send my best to John. Better yet, I'll give him a ring later on. It's been too long. I'm sure he would love to hear about the happenings in the neighborhood. Don't you?"

Samantha almost dropped her pocketbook. Samantha now knew without a shadow of a doubt that Elizabeth knew. Elizabeth knew and was toying with her.

Just as Samantha was about to say something, Elizabeth laughed out loud. She was enjoying herself. She had Samantha right where she wanted her.

At her mercy.

"Better yet, I know he's a busy guy and all. Maybe I'll call him another time. I don't want to interrupt your evening. Still, let him know I'm thinking of him. Send him our best. He's going to need it."

CHAPTER THIRTY-TWO

As Samantha settled in from her weekend, she couldn't believe what had transpired between her and Elizabeth. She wished she was back at Lauren's. A couple of bottles of wine and some girl talk with her best friends had really put her mind at ease. Keeping her troubles from her friends was rough though. She had wanted to spill to Lauren at least a dozen times.

Instead she allowed Lauren and Christie to tell her their internet dating horror stories and she soon stopped thinking about Derek or John. She laughed and danced to bad eighties music and watched corny chick flicks.

Leaving the girls was hard. There was a part of her that wanted to stay with them. Being single and having stories to share of bad dates sounded wonderful and easy. Sure, she had stories but they were not to be shared with anyone, ever. Never. Now she had to come home to this shit with Lizzie.

She hadn't heard from John though, which Samantha took as a good sign. If he had heard from Derek or Elizabeth, her phone would have been blowing up and considering he hardly called while on business trips, she was pretty sure he was still in the dark.

By now her husband had probably had forgotten about their fight before he left. Perfect, she thought, as Mom always said, "Feed them and fuck them," and that was exactly what Samantha had in mind. She had planned an evening with his favorite meal and her most sexy lingerie. Plus, if he did hear from the Millers, she would know by the look on his face when he walked in the door.

"John, you are getting so lucky later on when you get home!" She laughed, she was going to push her conversation with Elizabeth to the back of her mind and get ready for a fantastic evening with her husband.

Samantha went into full "Sexy time" preparation. They had had sex the night before their big fight, but Sam had felt nothing. It was the usual same position, the same motions, the same everything. It was good but it wasn't as satisfying as it was with Derek. At least the anticipation of sex with Derek was exciting. Knowing that the next day after sleeping with John she would be wrapped in Derek's arms in the middle of the day always made her feel fulfilled.

Tonight however she was going to bring back the excitement into her marriage. Maybe it was guilt sex, but Samantha didn't care, she needed to reassure John or maybe herself, and try and get Derek off her mind.

After putting the baked potatoes in the oven, she ran upstairs and pulled out her sexiest lingerie. Looking at the clock, she had roughly forty five minutes to get ready before John was expected home.

She slipped on her lingerie, put her hair up with a few tendrils hanging down the way John liked and for the final touch put on her thigh highs and garter belt along with her red fuck-me pumps. She looked in the mirror and was almost sick again. It occurred to her that she had worn this exact outfit for Derek once.

"Stop, Sam, this is for John. Derek was a mistake, a mistake that you keep making." She shook her head, took a look into the mirror and practiced her come hither smile. "Perfect."

CHAPTER THIRTY-THREE

The front door slammed shut and John came strolling into the kitchen where Samantha stood putting the final touches to dinner. John was smiling. She let out a sigh of relief, sensing that he had not heard from the Millers.

"Wow, now this is what I call a welcome home! What did I do or better yet, what do you want?" John tilted his head and narrowed his eyes.

"Oh John, I'm not looking for anything, drop the lawyer act for once. Can't a wife surprise her husband that she missed with his favorite meal and sexy lingerie?" Samantha wrapped her arms around his neck and gave her best come hither grin.

"And dessert?" John licked his lower lip and cupped the sides of Samantha's face.

"You get me." She tilted her head the best she could in the palms of John's hands and looked up at him through her long lashes.

He leaned in and they began to kiss. She fell into his embrace and he shifted towards the kitchen table. He lifted Samantha so she was perched on the edge of the table; she wrapped her legs around his hips. John had never been a spontaneous lover before so this sudden urge to make love in the kitchen took her by surprise; however she wasn't complaining. She was here with her husband who apparently had no idea about her love affair and she wanted to keep it that way.

Samantha pushed John's suit jacket over his shoulders down his back and let it fall to the floor. He traced his lips down his wife's neck while his fingers toyed with the clasp on her bra. "Dinner's going to have to wait."

As Samantha unbuttoned John's pants his cell phone rang, interrupting the moment.

She crossed her arms and pouted at him as he reached to answer it. "Do you have to get that now John?"

With a puzzled look on his face he hit the screen to answer, and whispered yes while turning to leave the kitchen. She couldn't help but let out a groan.

"John Bennett." Almost immediately his playful disposition changed; he looked back at Samantha and grimaced as he continued out and upstairs towards his office. Samantha tiptoed behind him to listen in. She could only hear his muffled voice through the closed door, but what she heard made her stomach sink.

"When did this happen?" What exactly are you saying? Are you positive?" John's voice was rising and she could hear how worked up he was getting.

Her ears began to ring. She darted back down into the kitchen where she reached on the countertop for support. Her hands started to shake. She had one thought only. Lizzie. He's on the phone with Lizzie. "Holy shit, what am I going to do? This can't be happening. I thought for sure she was making empty threats. Stupid bitch means business."

Samantha was beginning to feel dizzy as the tingling sensation ran through her body. Between the buzzing in her ears and her heart pounding, she was in fear of fainting. She leaned over the counter and grabbed a glass from the draining board. She let the faucet run a bit and splashed some cold water across her face before she filled the glass to sip. Now what? she thought. Immediately she was trying to think of her next move. *Would he leave? Would he divorce me? What would I do then? I'd have to find a job.* She saw her life unfolding in front of her. She saw everything they had worked for start to disappear. She heard the study door open and John's heavy feet padding down the stairs.

He stalked into the kitchen; he loosened his tie and undid the top two buttons of his shirt with one hand. He was livid and was about to blow. She noticed the vein in his neck throbbing and his face was flushed. She braced herself. "John, honey, what's wrong?"

He slammed his fist down on the kitchen table causing her to jump. "Are you fucking kidding me Sam? How could you do this to me?" His jaw clenched.

"Do what John? I'm confused." Trying to remain calm, she did her best to stand still, while her insides felt like a category five earthquake.

"I work my goddamn ass off all day for you, so you can have your designer shoes, and handbags. You don't have to worry about a goddamn thing." His words trailed off as he stroked the nape of his neck and turned away from her. "You're confused, really? How do you have the audacity to stand there and act all innocent?" He turned back around and made eye contact. "You can't bat your eyes out of this one Sam. Not this time."

Samantha's throat went dry. She tried to speak but nothing came out. She lifted the glass of water and took a sip, "Please, John hear me out." She stepped closer to him. She was desperate; she knew how angry he was and it frightened her. *This could really be it, what can I do?*

"You have no idea what kind of predicament you put me in. You had better hope I can resolve this. Jesus Christ Sam, this is my reputation you're messing with!" He was furious; no matter how upset he had been with Samantha in the past, he had never raised his voice at her the way he did now.

Tears started to fall from Samantha's eyes. She was trembling uncontrollably. She placed the water on the table with a thud and was about to throw herself at her husband's feet and beg for mercy. The words were on the tip of her tongue when she noticed an envelope in his hand that he had been holding since he came down from the office. She froze and couldn't take her eyes away. *What was in that envelope? Did he have proof of her affair with Derek? Photos maybe? How long has Elizabeth known about it, that she could send mail? Oh my god, this can't be happening to me right now.* Her hand went to her forehead, her breathing was heavy and short, panic set in and she fell to her knees crying out. "I'm sorry, please forgive me. John, don't leave me, I don't want to be alone, I'm so lonely, let me explain." She took in short breaths one after the other trying to catch that one deep breath but her body would not allow it. She continued to tremble and the tears continued to pour down her cheeks. She wiped at her nose with the back of her hands.

John stood staring at his wife in disbelief. He knelt down and wrapped his arm around her shoulder.

"Samantha." He lifted her chin up and kissed her forehead. "Honey, I'm sorry for the way I yelled, maybe I overreacted, but come on, calm down."

She looked up at him with confusion, "You did?" Her breathing began to slow, and her body stopped shaking.

"I asked you before I left to drop this off at FedEx." He placed the envelope down on the table along with his suit jacket. As he stood up he pulled Samantha up into his embrace. "It's the one thing I asked you to do. These are very important depositions that needed to be at my client's office. Samantha, how could you forget?" John let go of his wife and walked out of the kitchen to retrieve his briefcase from the front entry way; when he returned he placed it on the kitchen table opening it to sort through documents.

Relief hit Samantha. She wiped the rest of her tears away. "I am so sorry John. Is there any way you can fix my mistake? I don't know what happened." She cupped her face with both hands, taking in deep breaths.

"Sam, what were you talking about with leaving and being lonely?" He looked up from his briefcase staring at his wife.

"Babe, I'm not going anywhere; you may drive me crazy at times, but I'm not your father. I'm not going to just up and leave."

"It's nothing, really. I'm sorry, it's just you've been away a lot and it gets lonely, that's all. Forget I said anything. Is there someone you can call and get an extension? I feel terrible."

"I sure as hell hope so. You ok now?" John pulled out more documents from his briefcase and hesitated, before marching back up to the study. Samantha took a minute, pulled herself together and poured herself a glass of wine. *That was too much for me to handle, what am I doing? He's right, he may not be here all the time, but he does support me. I need to change my ways. From this day forward, new Sam!* She decided to grab her husband a beer and join him in the study. She needed to get a grip though. This whole affair with Derek had changed her; she needed to be stronger than ever now.

He looked up at her as she entered, a smile on his face. Samantha took that as a good sign and walked over to his desk. She placed his beer down next to him.

She strolled around the chair and started to massage his neck. She could feel his muscles loosen and his shoulders relax with her touch. She was definitely relieved; she had never been so petrified in her life. He hung up the phone while grabbing her hand with the other and kissed her fingers. He looked up over his shoulder at her.

"I'm sorry, honey. I shouldn't have gone off like that; I was able to get an extension, no worries. Let's take this back to our room and let me make it up to you." On any other given day

Samantha wouldn't have let him get away with his tirade so easily, but this time she carried so much guilt and was more relieved than anything, so she let him lead her to their bedroom.

"Hey, what's up with the Millers?" asked John, unbuttoning his shirt. "Their house looks vacant."

"What do you mean, vacant?"

"I noticed the porch furniture is gone. Looks like the window treatments were removed too, and all Elizabeth's hanging plants are gone."

A sudden rush of panic rose to the surface again. *Where is everything? Where are they?* She should have felt relieved but she felt sad. She felt unfinished. She also felt like she was going to be sick again. Taking a deep breath she pushed the vomit down and quickly adjusted the pillows on their bed. She had known deep down that the Millers would leave, but not so soon. *So, was that the "big plans" Lizzie mentioned? Better this way, right?* She thought. Still she felt a loss deep inside.

"How would I know?" Samantha replied shrugging her shoulders trying to act normal.

"It's odd, no? You spent more time with them than I did. They didn't say anything to you?" He looked at Samantha and continued to pull off his suit slacks and dress socks.

"No. Why would they? John, I don't really feel like discussing the Millers and their whereabouts. I just want to focus on us right now."

"I'm beginning to think you're scaring them away. What goes on around here while I'm at work?"

She shot him a look and rolled her eyes. "Whatever." She moved to the foot of the bed and rested one knee on the mattress. Samantha watched her husband finish undressing and put his shoes neatly away in their place.

"You think I should give Derek a call and see what's going on? I hope everything is alright." John removed his watch and placed it on the dresser with his cell.

"I think we need to worry about what we're doing or not doing at the moment." Samantha walked over to John as he was about to reach for his phone off the dresser. "This can wait. I can't." She took his hands and guided him over towards the bed. "Why don't you finish undressing already and wait for me. I'll be right back."

"Ok, it's getting late anyway, maybe I'll call tomorrow" He pushed himself back on the bed and folded his arms behind his head. Samantha sashayed her way into the master bathroom.

She closed the bathroom door, feeling sick again. She thought she might throw up. Not now, please not now. Let me freshen up and enjoy this evening with my husband. Samantha opened the bottom drawer hoping she would find some stomach medicine. Going through the drawer pushing things aside, there it was laying at the bottom of the drawer. Samantha slowly picked it up. Stunned and shocked she lifted the box out of the drawer and stared at it. Could it be? As early as ten days? There it was, the answer to her nausea, the moodiness, everything. This explained it all. Her hands shook as she opened the box. Deep down she knew; she had been through this before, she didn't even have to pee on the stick to confirm. She ripped the package open and took the test, then waited for the dreadful three minutes. Three minutes to confirm her suspicions. Sitting there staring at the stick starting to change color, she started to feel sick. Not because she was pregnant but because she now realized she had another problem.

She started to calculate the days inside her head from when she missed her period. According to her calculations she was about a week and half late. She became frantic as she tried counting back to the days she and John made love, but without a calendar she couldn't be certain. She was usually on top of keeping track of her ovulation, and when they tried to conceive, those days she would try to avoid seeing Derek, but her affair with him hadn't been just a few days here and there, they were pretty active. It had become a daily routine for them. Sometimes twice in one day, sometimes passion took over and well…She sat in bewilderment on the closed toilet lid. What could she do? This was her dream, having a baby, being a family. She hung her head in shame. *It serves me right, the one thing in life that means so much to me, and I can't even enjoy the moment.*

John knocked on the door. "Sam? You coming out? You've been in there for a few minutes. What's taking so long?"

Samantha couldn't think straight, she felt worse now than ever. What was she going to do? Should she wait and confirm the pregnancy with her doctor before telling John? But what if she had problems again? I can't wait, or delay the process. I'm pregnant. But who is the father? How could I have been so careless? What was I thinking? The stick rested on the sink counter screaming up at her. She closed her eyes tight to fight back the tears.

"What's this?" John pointed towards the pregnancy test, his face showing no expression.

Samantha was startled, she had been so distracted with her own thoughts, she never noticed John opening the bathroom door and coming in. She looked back and forth between the test and her husband. Looking baffled and confused, her husband stood there waiting for an answer. It was too late to cover it up. There was only one thing to do. She stood up and gave her husband a sheepish grin. "I guess you can say it's my fresh start."

THE TIMES TRILOGY

TIME of SORROW

◆ BOOK TWO ◆

"In times of joy and in times of sorrow..."

You can only hide the truth for so long, until your past comes back to haunt you...

Does Samantha's dream of having a baby come true, and if so, who is the father?

Will her skeletons be revealed and threaten everything she has built for herself?

Is this the last of the Millers?

Don't miss the continuing story of Samantha Bennett. Discover the secrets, deceptions and emotions that fuel her desires.

TIME of TRIUMPH
◆BOOK THREE◆

"In times of failure and in times of triumph..."

Stay connected for updates on the last installment of

THE TIMES TRILOGY

STAY CONNECTED WITH AMANDA AND STACIE

To learn the latest information regarding, Time of Want, Time of Sorrow, Time of Triumph, and other endeavors…

We can be found at our social media links. We would love to hear from you!

Facebook Author Page:

www.facebook.com/pages/Stacie-Jacobs-Amanda-Bianco/482562078546288

Facebook Book Series Page:

www.facebook.com/pages/Amanda-N-Stacie-Novelists/1551544685127427

Come Follow us on Twitter:

www.twitter.com/AmandaB_StacieJ

Add us on Goodreads:

www.goodreads.com/book/show/25353907-time-of-want

www.goodreads.com/user/show/32323344-amanda-bianco

www.goodreads.com/user/show/33538051-stacie-jacobs

ACKNOWLEDGEMENTS

Where should we begin? This book started out so many years ago, it was just something fun to do together and pass the time. With every chapter written, our excitement grew and we became more invested in these characters. We decided to move forward and publish our story.

It has been a long journey, but well worth it. We have been blessed to have so many good people on our side. First, we would like to thank our husbands, **MJ Bianco and Matt Jacobs** for all of their love and support. We know it wasn't easy at times, but you still supported us every step of the way. We love and appreciate all that you do for us.

To our children, **Robert Bianco, Marisa Bianco, and Dalton Jacobs** - No matter how old you are, or what obstacles you are presented with, you should always follow your dreams. It is never too late to make something happen. You just have to stick with it, and give it your best.

Beta-readers – Where would we be without any of you? We appreciate all of the feedback you have given, it was a long road, but with all of your input and support, we were able to bring our story to a much better place.

(Tina Sasso, Pam McComb, Alice Maurer, Arlene Zagas, Julie Matteo, Linda Esposito)

We want to thank our editor, ***Allison Williams***, for all of your help and knowledge. Thank you for believing in our story and helping us make it what it is today.

We just want to add a special thank you to ***Christopher Sasso***, and ***Julie Masoian***. We appreciate you taking the time to help give 'Time of Want,' one last final proofread.

Thank you ***Matt Jacobs*** for creating the perfect key for our cover. We know it wasn't easy at times dealing with the two of us!

We want to thank ***Lori Follett*** from ***Wicked Book Covers*** for seeing our vision and bringing our idea to life. You created such a fantastic book cover that we absolutely love and your suggestions, made it that much better. Working with you was such a pleasure.

ABOUT US

Amanda was born and raised on Long Island, New York, and still lives there with her husband of eight years, and two small children. Their son is six and daughter is two. After giving birth, she was fortunate enough to stay at home with her children. Amanda is the youngest of four girls, and loved growing up in a big family. Once she graduated high school, she started working in retail full time. She has always had a creative imagination, but her passion for writing only started a few years ago. The more she read, the more obsessed she became. Now, she loves to write and create stories that people will hopefully enjoy reading. A few of her favorite things to do are: listen to music, read, bake, and spend time with family.

Stacie was born and raised on Long Island, New York. She is the youngest of three girls. After high school, Stacie went to Dowling College and then to St. Joseph's college, with the hopes of being a teacher or speech pathologist. Her senior year, she became very ill and left. At the age of thirty two, she was diagnosed with severe rheumatoid arthritis. Wanting a change, Stacie relocated to Texas in 2006, and shortly after moving, she met her husband. Within six months, they married and now have a three year old son. They hope to complete their family with another baby soon. Now, being a stay at home Mom, Stacie has hopes of finishing her degree and to continue writing.

Amanda and Stacie have been friends for over twenty years. The first ten years, they worked in retail together, until they both decided to pursue other careers. The friendship has grown stronger over the years and no matter how far apart they live, it continues to grow. Amanda and Stacie have always made a great team.

Made in the USA
Middletown, DE
10 August 2015